Caught In The Frame

PONDEROSA PINES MYSTERIES
BOOK THREE

REGINA WELLING

ERIN LYNN

Willow Hill
BOOKS

Caught In The Frame

Contents

Chapter 1

"...**A**nd then he kissed me." Chloe LaRue paused for dramatic effect, remembering the way Nathaniel Harper's hands had tangled in her hair; the love that poured from his lips and sent her senses reeling. Twin sighs escaped the mouths of her two girlfriends, Veronica and Mindy, as they listened with rapt attention. Chloe relished the rare chance to gush about her up-until-recently non-existent love life.

A large pizza, so far untouched, rested on the coffee table, surrounded by an array of snacks that, if polished off in one night, would send all three of them into total sugar shock. Veronica sipped a bright pink cocktail through a makeshift Twizzler straw, her cornflower blue eyes opening wide over the rim as she absorbed every word of Chloe's story. Mindy sat stick-straight in a lotus position, her feet tangled, pretzel-like, in front of her. Chloe and Veronica were so used to the yoga instructor's mannerisms they barely noticed anymore when Mindy twisted herself into spontaneous poses at the oddest of times.

"What happened next?" Veronica wiggled her eyebrows suggestively, correctly deciphering the blush rising to stain Chloe's cheeks a delicate pink. She wouldn't—couldn't—let it go without ribbing her friend just a bit. After watching Nate and Chloe engage in a two-decade-long mating dance they had nicknamed the Will They, Won't They Waltz, Veronica and Mindy were delighted the pair had finally realized their true feelings for one another.

Pining for each other since puberty—but having lived most of that time on opposite corners of the world—the two of them had now permanently returned to the tiny town of Ponderosa Pines, making a long term relationship possible. However, miscommunication and a healthy dose of insecurity made the transition from *friends* to *more than friends* difficult, to say the least.

Chloe rolled her eyes and raised her right eyebrow at Veronica, shooting her friend a glance correctly interpreted as "Duh", and continued. "I haven't had enough of these to go into the gory details," she raised her glass for emphasis, "and I don't intend to. But, we definitely took our relationship to the next level. A couple of times." Chloe grinned sheepishly, and her friends dissolved into giggles.

Three short days ago, Nate had burst through her front door to officially declare his love. Chloe would have been quite content to continue spending every possible second since then devoted to memorizing the long lines of his spectacular body. Instead, reality and responsibility pried them out of their love nest, and forced Nate back to his assignment of training Ponderosa Pines' newest lawman. Rather than sit around and wait for him, Chloe had turned her phone back on, answered the dozen or so messages that had accrued on her voicemail, and acquiesced to an impromptu girls' night in.

As the last—or second-to-last, if you counted her very closest friend, EV Torrence—one of the group to lose her single status, Chloe couldn't deny the desire to *tell* someone about the incredible weekend she had just experienced. So what if they were all thirty-something, and probably too old to be giggling like school girls; you were only as old as you felt, and it still made them all happy to act like teenagers every once in a while.

Veronica, whose near-perfect marriage produced five beautiful, rambunctious children—and Mindy, childless by choice, but very much in love with her longtime boyfriend—were over the moon about the recent development in Chloe and Nate's relationship. Now, if only EV could sort out her own love life, all of Chloe's closest friends would be coupled up. Of course, EV had twenty years on the rest of them, so her situation was a bit more complicated than the others.

"You two can pull those canary feathers out of your mouths, by the way. EV already told me you were in on her little plot. Dragging me into situations where I'd have to see Nate was bad enough, but setting me up to date a bunch of losers and make Nate look like the better choice...jerks." Her grin showed she bore no malice. "I already knew he was perfect, I just let fear get the best of me."

"Should we expect retaliation?" Veronica smirked. "What you did to EV wasn't so different from what we did to you, Miss Pot Who Calls Kettles Black."

Chloe had to admit submitting her best friend's profile to an online dating service probably went a bit beyond nice. Yet, she defended herself, "As if EV's one to talk. She and Dalton are perfect for each other, and you can tell he's totally in love with her. Too bad she's still holding him at arm's length."

"That's not what I heard!" Mindy sing-songed. "There's a rumor going around that he was seen leaving her house after a torrid night of lust—at least that's what Lottie Calabrese's been telling everyone. Care to confirm?"

Chloe rolled her eyes but conceded, "Yes, it's true. But they hit another bump in the road, and still have a few issues to work out." How much should she tell them about recent developments?

Almost no one knew that former resident, Remy Vincent—who just happened to also be EV's ex—was suspect number one in Ponderosa Pines' first mystery of note. Unless the evidence lied, Remy had mastertminded an attempted coup that would have forced their beloved town into being dissolved and absorbed by neighboring Gilmore. Remy's blackmail attempt failed miserably when its victim, Evan Plunkett, turned up dead—murdered by the cuckolded husband of Evan's most recent paramour. Everyone knew that part of the story—just not that the shadowy figure attempting to play puppetmaster with their town had such close ties. Until

Remy was caught, EV and Dalton had agreed to put their budding relationship on hold—a decision Chloe thought bordered on the ridiculous. So what if Dalton's job as deputy meant he had to keep certain bits of evidence from EV? It wasn't like she told him everything either.

"I have every intention of lending a hand; what's good for the goose is good for the gander."

"Lending a hand?" Mindy practically snorted out the words. "You mean meddling in their business."

Chloe put on her best innocent look—Bambi eyes and all. "It's done out of love."

If EV had been completely happy as a vibrant, single woman, Chloe would have let the topic drop. And, until a recently-single Dalton came into the picture, a series of short-term relationships satisfied EV's occasional craving for companionship. Enter Nate's partner, the caring Deputy Dalton, and everything changed. For the first time since the disaster of Remy, EV let someone into her life who might just become permanent.

Unfortunately, Remy Vincent still stood between them. Suspecting she was at the heart of his vendetta against Ponderosa Pines, EV had pulled back from the relationship with Dalton. Until all that was laid to rest, they were in a holding pattern. Chloe sighed to herself, hoping silently that everything would work out in the end, and pushed the thought from her mind in order to focus on more pleasant matters.

"G'night, you guys." Chloe hugged first Veronica, and then Mindy. She watched them for signs of alcohol-induced impairment, saw none, and let them skip down her front steps to begin the short walk back to their own houses.

"Love you!" Veronica called over her shoulder.

Chloe glanced at the clock, which read 1:15 am, thought better of her plan to clean up the mess in her living room at a more reasonable hour, and grabbed the garbage can from the kitchen. The sudden trilling of her cell phone stopped Chloe in her tracks. Veronica and Mindy should be home by now, and who else would be calling at this hour? There was only one option that didn't have her worrying about the safety of everyone she held dear: Lila.

Her mother's cheerful "Hello, love" confirmed Chloe's suspicions that Lila had once again forgotten the time difference between Ponderosa Pines and whatever European country in which she was currently ensconced.

"Hi Mother, is everything okay? You're aware it's the wee hours of the morning here, right?"

"Everything is lovely, darling. You know I'm lousy with time conversions. Besides, this couldn't wait."

"There's an app for that." Chloe could hear the excitement in Lila's voice, and braced herself for an explanation.

Lila brushed the dry suggestion aside, "Javier proposed! I'm getting married in three weeks, and I want you and EV to come to Ireland and be my bridesmaids!" Chloe's stomach dropped. Heat born of concern rushed through her veins for a split second before reason won out and cooled the fire. It wasn't the first time Lila had enamored herself with a new man—most of them unsavory in some way. She seemed to attract men who only saw the shine and the money, but not the perfect heart underneath. But, this *was* the first time Lila had actually agreed to marry any of them, even though she had been proposed to more times than Chloe could count. You could feed a small country on the accumulated worth of Lila's rejected engagement rings.

What could this man possibly have that the

horde before him had lacked? Chloe wished she hadn't been so dismissive the last time Lila called; she knew she hadn't been paying any attention to her mother's description of Javier, believing that he'd be out of the picture soon enough. Now, she was left wondering what her soon-to-be *step-father*—Chloe cringed at the word—was like.

"Congratulations, Mom!" she replied brightly. If this was what Lila wanted, Chloe wouldn't take even one iota of her happiness away. At least not until she had good reason; soon enough, she would be there in person to watch closely and stop her mother from rushing headlong down the path toward disaster. "Of course, I'll come, and I imagine EV isn't going to miss it either. Do I get a 'plus one'?"

"*You* want to bring a date?" Lila's voice rose an octave, her incredulity evident even from across the Atlantic.

"Nate and I finally worked out our issues. We're officially a couple, and I think getting away from the prying eyes of everyone in town for a few weeks is just the thing we need. Of course, that is, if Javier doesn't mind Nate tagging along with him while we're attending to wedding details." A plan had already begun to form in her mind. Nate's assignment would be to spend time assessing the groom, while leaving Chloe and EV free to deal with Lila, and what was sure to be a spectacle of a wedding.

"Well, the sky must be falling. I didn't want to push the issue with you before, since you're so freaking *sensitive* about it, but I hoped you'd figure it out eventually. Of course, bring him along, darling. I'll overnight vouchers for all three of you. We're flying out tomorrow ourselves. Come as soon as you can; I can't wait to see you."

Bidding her mother goodbye, Chloe took a moment to get over the shock. She shook her head picked up the phone to dial EV's number before realizing it was now closing in on 2 o'clock in the morning. Though it would be fun to interrupt EV's sleep for once—her friend had a knack for waking Chloe at the butt-crack of dawn every chance she got—the news could wait until morning.

"Mom and I stayed there a number of times before. Castle Ligean is simply amazing—more a resort than a hotel—and they do a *lot* of weddings, so most of the planning part will amount to us reigning in Mother's over-the-top ideas." Sitting on her favorite section of EV's kitchen island, waiting for the jaunty red teapot to whistle, Chloe watched while EV perused the castle's website. From her perch, Chloe looked over EV's shoulder at the laptop on the coffee table, currently displaying an extensive slideshow of rolling Irish hillsides, sprawling grounds, and gleaming waterfront vistas.

"She's always had a penchant for the dramatic, that's for sure. Of course, she'd pick a castle in the middle of Ireland; wouldn't want to do anything halfway, that one." EV snorted from across the room. Once upon a time, Lila and EV had been inseparable—the best of friends. But when Lila had fled from the Pines as soon as Chloe was old enough to handle extensive travel, their bond had become somewhat strained. EV felt closer to Chloe, despite their age difference, than she ever had to Lila.

EV, who still lived in the house her parents had built, held a place of honor in their small community, having been instrumental in turning the once-hippie-commune into a legitimate town. Lila spent the last twenty years searching for something *more,* while EV chose to put down roots in Ponderosa Pines. Neither woman understood or fully respected the other's choices, which led to a give-and-take of subtle jabs that kept their relationship from ever returning to its unconditional beginnings. Two weeks spent in close proximity was either going to eliminate or solidify the emotional disconnect between them. Chloe hoped for the former, since these were the two most important women in her life.

"So we'll leave on Saturday. That gives us two weeks before the wedding. Seems doable."

Chloe leaned over to look at the website alongside EV.

"Ooh, look at the spa services. They've expanded the selection. You would love a mud bath. And we're definitely getting hot stone massages. And facials. Oh, this is going to be fun!"

"Have you lost your ever-loving mind? Look who you're talking to here. All I can picture is the Wash-Em Brush-Em team from Oz, scrubbing and buffing me 'til I'm shiny and new. Not happening. Maybe Nate will join you for that one." EV tried for a tone that suggested the topic wasn't up for debate, but softened at the mention of Nate's name. She was thrilled about Chloe and Nate's newfound happiness, and only approximately 10% of her joy was related to smugness at the fact that she had helped make it happen. Well, maybe 15%, but who was counting?

"I already have plans for us: Jacuzzi suite, couples

massages..." Chloe's expression took on a dreamlike quality, her voice trailing off as her thoughts flew to the inevitable conclusion of those activities.

EV plucked a throw pillow off the couch and flung it at Chloe's head. "If you are imagining Nathaniel Harper naked, just stop it right now!"

Chloe recovered quickly: the startled look on her face replaced with mock-vengeance, she bounced down from the counter and lobbed the pillow back across the living room, where EV quickly snatched it out of the air.

"What about 'Babble & Spin'? Have you talked to Wesley about that yet?" EV was referring to Chloe's gossip column in the small Ponderosa Pines weekly newsletter, *The Pine Cone*. She couldn't exactly keep up with the goings-on at the Pines from halfway across the globe, and readers would certainly notice if the most popular article was missing for several weeks.

There was a good reason Chloe couldn't allow anyone in town to make a correlation between the column's absence and her travel plans: she was the latest in a series of anonymous authors of 'Babble & Spin'. The quirky, beloved tradition was just one of the little things that made the Pines special; people enjoyed speculating about the mystery as much as they enjoyed the gossip itself.

Nobody, save for EV—with her borderline-magical deductive skills—knew that Chloe was the columnist, not even Nate. The last thing Chloe wanted was to become the first author in the history of the paper to be outed.

A contingent of townspeople had EV pegged for the role, since nothing happened in the Pines without her knowing something about it. Given that, it wasn't a long leap to assume she had something to do with the column, but EV preferred to tend the gossip vines on her own. Though she enjoyed feeding information to Chloe, EV had no desire to take up the post herself.

"I'm toying with some ideas on how to sidestep suspicion, and I'm meeting him at his office later to discuss options." Wesley's office consisted of an artfully re-purposed storage pod occupying a corner of his backyard. Chloe didn't frequent the space, keeping her distance, since she had no official affiliation with the *Pine Cone* besides the occasional editorial piece submitted under her real name.

EV continued browsing through the wedding section of the castle's website, noting the myriad of expensive-looking options for the discerning bride. Full service was an understatement: of course, their five-star restaurant would provide catering, and a spectacular cake; the salon would cover hair, makeup, nails, etc. Above and beyond, the resort employed a full-time photographer, florist, seamstress—even an ice sculpture artist—not to mention, a staff of professional event planners who could make even the biggest Bridezilla's dreams come true. EV guessed that if Lila had wanted acrobats to fly across the banquet hall pouring champagne, the Castle Ligean staff would find a way to accommodate the request.

Letting a low whistle escape her lips, EV promised herself that if she did ever get hitched, she'd make it easy on everyone and skip the diamond-encrusted path through wedding hell. *Vegas all the way,* she vowed.

Sugar and Spice, the names much too mild for the antics of Chloe's pair of Siamese kittens, wreaked pandemonium every time Nate walked into the house. They'd taken an instant liking to the man, who gave them warm snuggles and unending chin scratches. Now, the sound of something crashing to the floor—most likely something from a shelf the kittens knew was off limits—let Chloe know he had just stepped through the front door. Shaking her head over the possible loss of another tchotchke, Chloe didn't move to greet him. Instead, she lounged on her bed, clad in a hot pink babydoll nightgown that threatened the line between sexy and slutty. Chloe had spent a solid hour wrapping her long, flowing blond hair in curlers to achieve a soft, wind-blown look. Her bright, almond-colored eyes were sheathed by long, thick lashes; her full lips coated in a shiny, but not sticky, gloss.

"In here!" She called, as Nate searched the front rooms to no avail. When he wandered into the bedroom doorway and almost dropped a purring Sugar in surprise, Chloe knew how squarely she had hit her mark. As her eyes raked over his adorably-messy chestnut hair, to his strong, scruffy jaw, and down his sculpted, muscular body, she couldn't help but feel like the luckiest woman on earth. She knew, after the ordeal they had endured in order to be with one another, that he felt the same.

No words were necessary, but a strangled *wow* sighed from him before Nate sprang onto the bed and began kissing her breathless. Her hands tangled in his hair as she pulled him close, all other thoughts forgotten as she focused solely on the perfect man she couldn't stop touching. An hour and a half later, when they emerged from the bedroom in search of sustenance, Chloe remembered she had news of great importance to impart.

"There was a late night...well, technically an early morning development, and I've got news." Chloe figured Nate would be willing to attend Lila's wedding, but wasn't sure if, with his work schedule, it was realistic for him to take an extended vacation. It hurt to think of him anywhere but by her side; they had wasted too much time being stubborn, and she didn't relish the idea of being separated from him now. Not to mention that, even though they had been friends for years, it might be too early in their relationship to broach the subject of a lengthy vacation that included her mother.

Having lived practically in each other's pockets as children, Chloe and Nate's relationship as friends meant he and Lila were familiar with each other on those terms. It was one thing, though, to be Nate—the kid who does stuff with your daughter, and quite another to be Nate—the man who *does stuff* with your daughter. That he might not be ready for that partic-ular scenario was just hitting her now.

Nate looked concerned as a flash of uncertainty scrolled across Chloe's face. "What news?" he asked with trepidation.

While Chloe explained everything, from Lila's phone call down to the worry that inviting him to tag along was premature, Nate's expression morphed through surprise to excitement, and finally amusement. "Love, I have been waiting for and wanting this for a very long time. It doesn't feel too soon to me; of course, I'll go! Give up a chance to spend two weeks in an Irish castle with you, just because we haven't technically been together for very long? Not gonna happen; I'm in."

Relieved, Chloe threw her arms around Nate's neck and gave him another lingering kiss. "What about work, though?"

"Dalton can handle things around here, and I'll put the Gilmore department on alert; it'll be fine. Nothing bad ever happens in Ponderosa Pines, right?"

Chloe snorted at that. The recent murder of Evan Plunkett had taken the shine right off the town's unofficial motto.

"Good. Because boy, do I have plans for us! Massages, Jacuzzi suite, hiking, a couple of day trips. We're going to have an amazing time!"

"I imagine we'd have an amazing time if we never left the room." Nate flashed a mischievous grin and cocked an eyebrow; the implication, and the fact that he looked dead sexy doing it, caused a ripple of desire to run from the top of Chloe's head to the tips of her pink-painted toenails.

"Of that, I'm sure. Which is why I booked us an extra week at a private cottage in Galway after this is all done." Chloe's satisfied grin was answered with a gaping one from Nate, who did a little dance, picked Chloe up, and spun her around in a circle.

"I freaking love you!" He practically shouted, then threw her over his shoulder, Chloe's laughter trailing behind as he headed back to the bedroom.

Chapter 2

If she had her way, EV Torrence would send Murphy *and* his stupid law straight down the intention-paved road to hell where they belonged. Why was it when Dalton Burnsoll was the last person on earth she wanted to see, he seemed to be lurking around every corner, but when she actually needed to talk to him he pulled a disappearing act worthy of Houdini?

Even considering her lack of experience at relationships—and their present status as a quasi-couple —EV knew full well there was a rule against not telling him in person she had just made plans to fly halfway around the world. Tracking him down before someone else clued him in that she'd be spending the next two weeks in Ireland had launched her into what felt like a game of Whackamole.

There was no doubt Chloe had already spoken to Mindy and Veronica, which meant the information was well on its way though the town grapevine. Growling in frustration, EV hit speed dial for the second time. When his phone went to voicemail again, she debated whether she was annoyed enough to just text him and be done with it, or to go out looking for him.

Technically, she was a free agent, since they'd agreed to put their relationship on hold while they dealt with the nasty situation involving Remy Vincent. Technically, she didn't have to report to Dalton Burnsoll—or anyone else—if she wanted to go out of town. Technically didn't mean squat, though, because the man mattered to her.

Knitting bag slung over one broad shoulder, EV directed her long legs down the path toward town. Chilled November air turned each breath into a cloud of vapor as she picked up her pace from a frost-crunching walk to a slow jog. Delicate shards of frozen dew lay like powdered fairy dust over every blade of grass, every tree branch. When the sun broke through the scud of high clouds, it turned the world into a white, glittering glory that both dazzled the eye and made her thankful she had decided to walk.

Her town, Ponderosa Pines, was a place of beauty in every season. Well, maybe not mud season—the two or three weeks when spring thaw turned rich soil wet and sloppy. Right now, on the cusp of winter, these days where the town lay under a coating of sparkling ice crystals always touched something in her. She'd traveled plenty, but had yet to find any view comparable to watching the seasons dress this small town in colors from spring greens so tender they made her jaw ache, to today's diamond-dressed white.

Honestly, the timing for this trip couldn't have been worse. After two months of relative chaos, her life still wasn't completely back to normal—and wouldn't be until the investigation into Remy Vincent's activities was finally concluded. What he had hoped to gain with his blackmail scheme, she couldn't understand. Most crimes, according to every good mystery book, were committed for one of three reasons; love, money, or revenge. On that point, EV fully concurred.

Of the three, love was the wild card, often inter-twined with the other two. Given Remy's extended absence, money had seemed the most likely moti-vator until a thorough investigation proved none of the three parties involved—Gilmore, Ponderosa

Pines, or Remy—stood to gain anything in a monetary sense.

Boasting just over the minimum number of residents to qualify for town status, some 560 souls called Ponderosa Pines home. That number included pets and farm animals. From its humble beginnings as a commune in the sixties, one thing never changed—the dedication of every resident to living gently on the land. By town charter, each home or business must be constructed using a portion of recycled materials, and must also satisfy elevated codes for energy efficiency.

To the novice eye, homes built from alternative means—cordwood, rammed earth, straw bales, recycled tires, and even underground bunkers—looked like a crazy collection of rustic backwoods junk. However, underneath the town's simple exterior beat the heart of innovation. Cutting edge solar and wind technology powered the entire town with plenty to spare, but not enough to become a cash cow worth exploiting.

That left revenge. On a whole town, though?

Pondering that question, EV hit the end of the trail. A quick glance showed Dalton's truck in its customary spot in front of the small office he currently shared with Nate. She'd forgotten about him. Now that Chloe and Nate had finally gotten out of their own way and become an item, he was the weakest link in the gossip chain to Dalton.

In the rush to get this whole thing over with, EV stepped into the office without preamble. She'd no more than cleared the door when a triangle of folded paper bounced off her chest. Startled, she looked up to see sheepish grins mirrored on the faces of two grown men who'd been playing paper football during their working day.

"Don't let me interrupt the playoffs," her gaze fell on Dalton. "I can see this is more important than answering your phone."

The size of the office left little room for guest seating; EV was too keyed up to sit anyway, so she remained just inside the door, shifting from one foot to the other.

Dalton reached over to pluck a rice-filled plastic zipper bag from the shelf next to his desk. He shook the bag to reveal his phone amid the white grains. "My phone got wet." From the way his eyes landed everywhere but on hers, she assumed there was a longer, and probably unflattering story to go along with the bald statement.

He didn't offer details, so she blurted out in a rush, "I wanted to tell you I'm going to Lila's wedding. I'm sure Nate already told you." She glowered at the man in question, "but I wanted you to hear it from me." Hot blood rushed to her cheeks. She'd rather stick her arm in a bag of rattlesnakes than try to follow the tangled threads of her emotions when it came to Dalton Burnsoll. Right now, she couldn't remember which one of them had suggested putting their relationship on hold for the time being.

"Thank you for letting me know." The words sounded stilted and stupid to Dalton, but they were the best he could do at the moment, so he turned the conversation to the work aspect. "Nate will be in constant contact; I'll stay here to hold down the fort and tug what few lines we have on Remy. If I don't see you again before you leave..." Dalton stood, reached to give her a hug, but halfway there thought better of it and lamely patted her arm instead. He cleared his throat to finish the statement, but nothing came out.

"I'll let you get back to *work,* then." EV injected a healthy dose of sarcasm into the word, but softened the rebuke with a tentative smile. With a few notable exceptions, Ponderosa Pines was pretty quiet from a law enforcement standpoint. Dalton could easily handle things while they were gone.

Late to knitting group after her detour into Awkwardville with Dalton, EV took a seat beside Chloe, whose nimble fingers worked a flashing set of needles to produce stitch after perfect stitch. It was enough to make EV want to stab her own eye out. Chloe smirked when EV pulled the elephant gray blob of inexpertly rendered work from her bag. "Laugh it up, Missy, but this is going to be your Christmas present." EV muttered.

"What's it supposed to be?" Chloe asked with a pained expression on her face. "Looks like a pile of gargoyle crap."

"It's a hat."

"Well, you should shoot it and put it out of its misery." Chloe grinned. The truth was, if EV gave her the hat, Chloe would wear it. That's what you did when your best friend made something for you. Even if it was the ugliest garment in the history of knitting.

"Keep it up, and I'll make you a matching pair of mittens."

Priscilla Lewellyn's quiet chuckle did not go unnoticed, but it was her outfit that earned her a raised eyebrow from EV. Owner of Thread, the fabric store where knitting group was held, Priscilla's everyday wardrobe consisted of items worked by her own hand—generally using specialty yarns with a fuzzy or nubby texture. Today's dress, exquisitely crafted from variegated boucle yarn in a mix of fall colors, would have been fine on its own. It was the addition of some sort of collar apparatus that made the outfit go wrong. Ruffled around the edges, it looked like an old fashioned doily knit from the feathers pulled off of a wild pheasant. From that bit of fluff rose Priscilla's slim-to-the-point-of-skinny neck, which, along with her prominent nose, conjured the vision of a Thanksgiving turkey in EV's head. It wasn't the most charitable of thoughts, and yet she couldn't shake the image.

"Speaking of mittens," Talia Plunkett took the opportunity to change the subject, "I was thinking it might be a good idea to add a few pairs of stockings to the borrow boxes this year." The borrow boxes, a Ponderosa Pines innovation, held books for trade during summer months, and hats, mittens, and scarves during the winter—no trade necessary. "I'd be happy to donate several pairs to kick things off."

With a little too much time on her hands after her

husband's accidental death, Talia had turned to knitting. With a vengeance. Now she had a plastic tote filled with two dozen pairs of orphaned stockings.

"How is that speaking of mittens?" Talia's sister, Lottie Calabrese, sneered.

"Shut up, Lottie." Luther's death had somehow shortened Talia's patience and strengthened her spine. Once inclined to kowtow to her sister's acid tongue, she now waded in with a will. Stories of their epic public battles were gaining legendary status.

To stop this one in its tracks, Chloe blurted, "EV and I are leaving for Ireland on Wednesday. We'll be gone for a couple of weeks."

Her ploy worked; requests for more information bombarded Chloe.

"My mother's getting married." She tried for cheerful, but couldn't quite keep the edge of disgust from her tone. "Some guy she met a few months ago. Javier something or other."

"Tell her I hope she'll be very happy." Priscilla chirped. "It's too bad she never comes home."

"Well, she would, if EV would just cooperate." Waggling eyebrows followed by doe-eyed innocence met EV's pointed glare.

All eyes turned toward EV who, to her great

embarrassment, blushed. "Lila has vowed not to set foot in Ponderosa Pines until she can attend my wedding to Dalton."

A chorus of female *whoo* noises erupted.

"Is that a possibility?" The light of creative genius danced in Priscilla's eyes and EV pictured herself walking down the aisle in some knitted fantasy of a dress. Trouble was, most of Prissy's creations tended toward her own tastes, and EV really didn't fancy looking like Mother Goose. That this was her biggest worry, and not the actual idea of marrying Dalton—or anyone for that matter—escaped her notice entirely.

"Considering we've been on two dates, I think you can hold off on renting the hall just yet."

"Three," Chloe corrected, earning a lifted eyebrow from EV. "If you consider a night of torrid passion a date, then that makes three." The blush intensified.

"Two—three, doesn't mean anything." EV changed the subject to something that didn't make her feel shivery with dread and anticipation at the same time: the town Yule celebration. She rummaged through her yarn bag before pulling a spiral bound notebook from where it had slid to the very bottom;

yarn tangled through the binding. Several seconds passed while she freed the book, stuffing the offending strands back into the mess. EV tossed the notebook onto the coffee table. "Can I count on you ladies to take care of things while I'm gone?"

Lottie's eyes lit with anticipation. A self-styled decorating diva, she itched to put her own spin on one of the town's most-loved traditions. With two recent deaths and an invasion of Sasquatch hunters behind them, the town could use a little fun and cele-bration. Lottie and Talia went for the book at the same time, but it was Allegra Worth who snatched it from the table first.

When Allegra's husband killed Evan Plunkett for sleeping with his wife, everyone expected Allegra to leave town in shame. Instead, she had not only stayed, but shed much of her haughty demeanor and become even more involved with her neighbors.

"You two will fight over everything, and nothing will get done." It was no less than the truth. "I'll take point on this one." She turned entreating eyes toward EV. "You can count on me."

"Text or email if you have questions," and EV left it at that.

"Take care of my babies." Chloe murmured to

Talia, who had, along with her new obsession with knitting, begun a slow descent into crazy cat lady territory. In fact, Sugar and Spice were two of Talia's rescue kittens—forced, lovingly, onto Chloe by the only person she would tolerate such insolence from —EV. Fortunately, Chloe had fallen in love with the two rascals, though she suspected they were more crazy about Nate than they ever had been about her. Not that she could blame them.

Chloe struggled up Talia's front walkway; a cat carrier in one hand, a bag of supplies in the other. The task would have been simple if both kittens hadn't crawled to the very back of the enclosure, upsetting the handle's center of gravity. Talia reached for it, pulling the two angry kittens from their prison. Sugar made a beeline for her favorite perch: a stone shelf set high into the living room fireplace.

"We'll be juuust fine, won't we, luvvie?" Talia asked Spice; his ears flattened disdainfully in response to the baby talk. Neither kitten seemed thrilled to be shuffled back to Talia's cat menagerie, but Chloe knew Talia was the only person who wouldn't mind taking them for the near month-long period she would be away.

"Thanks a mil, Tallie. You're a life saver."

"You can thank me by taking as many photos of this shindig as you can manage. The whole town's jealous we can't come along. I'm guessing it will be quite the event."

Chloe grimaced. "That's what I'm afraid of. And let me know about anything juicy that goes on here. A few months ago, I wouldn't have bothered asking, but if all hell breaks loose again, I want to know about it." The request deflected all suspicion of Chloe as the resident gossip columnist, while still keeping her finger on the pulse of current events.

"Will do. Be safe. Have fun." Talia gave Chloe a friendly hug and sent her on her way. When Luther was alive, Talia had barely given her the time of day, which might have also been due, in part, to Chloe maintaining a slightly standoffish attitude for a time. Things had changed, and for the better, in Chloe's opinion. She just wished it hadn't had to come at such a cost.

Word must have traveled quickly once EV's neighbor, Celia, spied Nate loading a considerable amount of luggage into the back of the co-op's conversion van. By the time they had made it the half mile into town, and stopped at The Mudbucket for one last cup of coffee, at least ten townspeople were gathered to bid all three of them farewell. Chloe could imagine the series of texts that had daisy-chained down the block to pinpoint their location.

"Take good care of her." Horis slapped Nate on the back. Chloe couldn't help but grin; Horis, with his bottle-bottom glasses and signature Fu-Manchu mustache, was an unlikely, but solid friend. When a pile of firewood showed up on her porch with no note, or her bird feeders went from empty to mysteriously full, she knew it was Horis looking after her. Chloe wrapped her arm around his waist and gave him a quick squeeze while Nate shook his hand and replied with a wide smile of his own. "Of course, man."

Lottie sidled up to EV, whispering in her ear, "I'll keep you in the gossip loop while you're away; wouldn't want you to miss any of the *babble*." EV rolled her eyes and thanked Lottie for the sentiment. *That was thinly veiled.* She got a kick out of it when certain people assumed EV was the current voice of gossip for 'Babble & Spin'.

After receiving a dozen requests for photos and videos, Dalton was finally able to corral the group back into the van. "Sheesh, you'd think you all are going off to war. It's just a couple of weeks."

Something in his voice let EV know that it was going to feel much longer for Dalton, who would have to find another paper football partner to help him pass the time while Nate was away. She felt a twinge of regret at not asking him to come along, but things were complicated enough as it was. She let him curl his warm fingers around her own while Chloe and Nate, cuddled up together on the middle seat, watched with growing satisfaction.

Chapter 3

Neither Chloe nor EV were strangers to international travel; in fact, their carry-on essentials were so similar that when EV pulled out a plush neck pillow covered in bright red fleece, Chloe couldn't help but reach for her matching hot pink one with a twinkle in her eye. Nate, seated on the aisle next to Chloe, watched with interest until she offered him a navy blue version that had arrived by second-day delivery just in time for the trip. His answering grin was thanks enough for her.

"Great minds think alike." EV smirked.

The red-eye flight had them leaving Boston at midnight, and arriving in Dublin at 5pm local time. Thankfully, Lila had sprung for a non-stop flight, allowing them time to sleep and avoid excessive jet-lag. Twelve hours in the air was enough to jangle anyone's nerves, but the first-class accommodations made it much more pleasurable than any flight Nate had ever taken. When the stewardess asked if anyone wanted a hot towel, Nate accepted, although he didn't know exactly what he was supposed to do with it.

The only thing to tarnish the experience of flying in style was a scene caused by a minor celebrity, who thought his fifteen minutes of boy band fame required him to drink excessively and shout, "Show me your boobs," at random intervals and to no one in particular. When an aging comedian finally stood up and flashed an impressive set of the male variety, half the cabin cheered while the other half exchanged scandalized glances. EV and Chloe indulged in quiet speculation over whether he was a B or a C-cup. After that, the trip was uneventful.

EV spent the beginning of the flight playing peek-a-boo with the adorable and incredibly well-behaved five-year-old girl, Lizette, who occupied the seat ahead of her. By the time sleep overtook the tot, she had scaled her seat and was firmly ensconced on EV's lap, where they both snoozed for a good few hours.

In Dublin, the transfer from plane to train almost went off without a hitch. Little Lizette had decided EV was her new best friend, and pitched a tantrum of epic proportions when she discovered they would be parting ways. Screams shriller than a whistling teakettle echoed through baggage claim, while Lizette's mother, chagrined and apologetic, finally carried her outside.

Twice in the airport—once in customs, and once as they were leaving—EV felt a tingling twitch at the base of her spine signaling that someone was watching her. Remaining casual, she let her gaze roam over the crowd. Seeing nothing, she decided it was just the after-effects of a long flight. And they still had a train ride ahead of them. At this point, all she wanted was a hot shower and a few hours in a soft bed.

Chloe spotted Lila the moment their train pulled into the station. A white silk couture jumpsuit hung across her slim hips, tapering at the ankle just above a pair of exquisite, cobalt blue Louboutin suede booties. The ruffled, plunging neckline left room for a diamond necklace that would have sparkled enough to blind a person had the sun not already begun to set. It matched the engagement ring on Lila's left hand perfectly, and even more baubles dangled from her wrists and ears. Her handbag screamed Louis Vuitton, and the black cashmere peacoat draped across her arm probably cost more than Chloe's entire wardrobe combined. Lila's striking appearance was so out of place against the dingy platform, it would have been hard *not* to notice her.

The look of anticipation on Lila's face softened the severity of her outfit. She liked pretty, expensive things, but there was a Piniac in there somewhere; if she had seen someone in need, the coat would have gone home with them without a second thought. Chloe had always considered her mother a woman of contradictions. To some, she was a pleasant surprise —those people were usually expecting a hard, unfeeling snob—to others, particularly those in her social sphere who *were* genuine snobs, she was an oddity. Love her or hate her—there was no in-between when it came to Lila LaRue.

"Go, I'll get our things." Nate gestured for Chloe to move on ahead, having watched her excitement grow exponentially the closer they got to their destination. She kissed him on the cheek and made a beeline for the exit before anyone else had moved from their seat, nearly flying from the bottom step into her mother's waiting arms.

"Oh, darling, I've missed you so much!" Lila enveloped Chloe in a fierce hug, inhaling her daughter's familiar scent with a beatific expression on her face—a face so similar to Chloe's it was a little bit creepy. Blond hair hung in perfectly-coiffed ringlets, just skimming a pronounced collar bone, and wide almond-colored eyes shone bright above a button nose. EV and Nate watched through the train windows, in no hurry to interrupt the reunion between mother and child.

EV's stomach rumbled with nervous energy; it had been ten years since she and Lila set eyes on one another, and their relationship had wandered into stasis somewhere between acquaintance and friend. Why Lila had chosen her to be in the wedding at all was a mystery EV planned to solve. Until now, the thought of seeing her long-lost friend had been more abstract than concrete, so she avoided dwelling on it.

With Nate bringing up the rear, EV exited the train and stepped tentatively toward Lila, who rushed forward to greet her with no trace of hesitation. Apparently, Lila had chosen to ignore the emotional distance that stretched between them after years of physical distance. If her impressions were correct, Lila harbored a touch of resentment over EV's close friendship with Chloe, while, at the same time, feeling gratitude that someone was there to look out for her daughter.

On the flip side, EV thought Lila's moratorium on visiting her daughter harsh, and had not been shy in speaking her feelings. Still, she was more than willing to let it all go, especially if Lila had done the same.

"Look at us! We're old!" Lila laughed, though neither looked anywhere close to their actual ages. Lila's good humor was infectious, and EV felt the tension release from her shoulders.

"I'm not old, I'm travel-worn." EV arched an eyebrow and matched it with a sardonic smile.

Nate approached the three women, looking to Chloe for support. "Mother, you remember Nate."

"Hello Mrs.—Ms. LaRue." He stammered. "It's nice to see you again. Congratulations, and thank you for inviting me." Nate reached out as if to shake Lila's hand.

"Hello, Nathaniel." She replied, ignoring his hand and letting go of Chloe long enough to give him a short, but reassuring hug. "Call me Lila. It's much easier. And you're very welcome. We're happy to have you all here." Nate detected the hint of an edge to the words. The feeling solidified as Lila donned her coat and slung her arms around Chloe and EV's necks, leading them toward a black limousine idling in the parking lot, while he was left to help the driver handle the luggage. The speculative look she tossed back at him over her shoulder told him the move was intentional.

Once they were en route, Lila pulled a bottle of champagne out of the limousine's built-in chiller and proposed a toast. "To family, friends who are considered family, and those who may someday become family."

Nate toasted, wondering again if Lila placed intentional emphasis on a particular phrase; it sounded almost as if she'd be betting against him becoming a permanent fixture in Chloe's life. He shook his head, wondering if the stress of travel had him imagining things.

"You're all just going to love this venue. Chloe knows, since we've visited the castle before, and it just seemed like serendipity when Javier suggested it. The whole event came into focus, and I could picture the four of us gliding down that staircase in the Rose Room. You remember my cousin Faith, don't you? She'll be my third attendant, but she can't make it until next week. I just hope it's enough time to get her dress altered." Lila prattled on, but Chloe interrupted her, having latched onto a nugget of information she didn't want to let pass.

"So Javier is the one responsible for choosing one of the most remote locations in your repertoire. You couldn't find anywhere more out of the way, could you? Where is his family from? Are they all flying in for the ceremony?"

"Of course, dear. You don't think they'd miss the wedding, do you?" Lila's didn't elaborate on the details, but instead launched into another monologue about the wedding.

"Sounds like we'll be busy little bees for the next two weeks." EV intoned with an internal sigh. It was beginning to sound like she wouldn't have time to explore the countryside as planned, and resigned herself to being bored to tears by centerpiece arrangements and debates about proper garter placement. *If I survive two weeks of this, I should get a prize,* she thought. *If I haven't done away with Lila by then, I'll be eligible for sainthood.*

Pulling up to the place, Nate, wide eyes staring out the window, let loose a whistle. EV concurred.

Some genius of an architect had gone to a lot of trouble extending the existing structure with enough new construction to almost triple the original square footage. From the outside, it looked like a scene from a fairy tale. Turrets soared into the sky, castellated battlements ranged like gapped teeth across walls of ancient stone. EV's imagination ran wild trying to picture what lurked behind ponderous arched doors of aged wood and hinges beaten from bars of iron.

Despite living humbly in Ponderosa Pines, EV was no stranger to opulence. Her family was every bit as wealthy as Lila's. She had just chosen a simpler life, knowing full well what the alternatives were. Still, EV goggled when she got her first glimpse inside. Instead of a great hall, dank in the corners where flickering torchlight couldn't reach, the doors opened into a gleaming interior of polished stone sparkling under soft lighting provided by fixture after swanky fixture. Burnished bronze and alabaster-shaded sconces lined the walls, while a crystal-bedecked chandelier dominated half the ceiling area.

To her right, the concierge desk, clad in pretty pink marble, rested next to a bank of elevators. On one corner, a sleek white cat surveyed the new arrivals with eyes the color of polished jade. Of its own volition, her hand lifted to give the regal beast a scratch behind the ears. He rewarded her efforts with a loud purr while her eyes took in the rest of the lobby. Just ahead, a sculptural sweep of gleaming granite stairs gracefully curved toward what looked like a second-floor balcony running around three sides of the foyer. EV knew from the website that a hair salon, several boutiques, and a five star restaurant resided there. Just past the concierge area, propped-open glass doors provided access to a gift shop. Nearly anything you might need for your vacation could be found somewhere in the castle.

An impeccably crafted sign reading *Pub and café* swung from a wrought iron hanger on her left, and another, smaller sign indicated that the entrance to the spa was somewhere behind a huge staircase opposite the eatery.

As though reading the thoughts running through EV's mind, Chloe nudged her with an elbow and whispered, "Low voltage LEDs. Trust me."

That was all she had time to say before the concierge, a gentleman who bore an uncanny resemblance to Dame Christie's description of Hercule Poirot, spied Chloe.

"Miss LaRue, it's so good to see you." EV stifled a smile when the man's deep southern American accent and exaggerated lisp drove the good detective right out of her head. "And Miss Lila, just look at the two of you, together again. Such beauty in one place, why, it's a sight for these sore eyes." His eyes didn't look particularly sore, but they did slide ever-so-subtly toward Lila, as though searching for approval. "Leave your bags right here; I'll see they're taken up to your rooms. Now, I'm sure Miss Lila would prefer to show you the way, since your suite adjoins with hers. She wanted to keep all her ladies close during this time of preparation."

"Thank you Antoine." Lila, leaving Nate no choice but to follow, latched onto Chloe's arm on one side, and EV's on the other, practically dragging them toward the grand staircase. EV raised an eyebrow at the name. To be sure, he looked like an Antoine, but he sounded more like a Billy Bob. The cat spilled from the desk to prance along behind the three women, all the way up into the lofty reaches of the castle. It seemed EV had made a new friend.

When Nate moved to follow Chloe, Antoine called him back, "Mr. Harper, if you could come with me, please. I'll show you to your rooms."

"He's with me, Antoine," Chloe pulled away from Lila, turned back to tuck her hand into the crook of Nate's elbow.

"Miss Lila chose special accommodations for Mr. Harper."

Chloe treated her mother to a questioning glare.

"It's fine Chlo. I'll find you later." He dropped a peck on her cheek while keeping his eyes trained on Lila, who regarded the scene with equanimity. "Go. Spend time with your mother. It's been awhile since you've seen *her*." Whether he was meant to be the referee in some private mother-daughter war, or a pawn to be sacrificed on the playing field, Nate sensed no overt personal hostility from Lila. This was a power struggle that probably had nothing to do with him, and he would only involve himself in if it looked like Chloe needed the extra support—though he saw no harm in letting Lila know his position, which was firmly seated on Chloe's side.

Made it safe, jet-lagged and sleepy. Kiss the kittens for me. Chloe's text to Talia was preemptive; she knew Tallie would worry if she didn't check in, and hoped she'd spread the word and spare Chloe a few panicked calls from other friends, neighbors, and general busybodies.

Deciding to complete the task to the fullest extent, she sent a group message to Veronica and Mindy as well: *Touched down, safe and sound in my room—far away from Nate, thanks to my mother. Apparently, my dry spell is destined to resume.*

Moments later, her phone dinged with three replies.

Glad to hear it, have fun, kittens are fat and happy.—Tallie.

There must be some secluded areas in that place—could be interesting.—Min.

Get it, girl. You'll figure something out. Keep us posted!—V.

Chloe grinned; maybe they were right. Surely, she and Nate could carve out some alone time, even if that meant a little sneaking around was in order. Now that she thought of it, some clandestine cuddling might even be fun.

Chapter 4

More soft pink marble—illuminated by the light of what seemed like a thousand flickering candles—formed an intricate, curved pathway into the castle's spectacular oval-shaped dining room. A full wall of windows reflected the scene back onto itself, making the room appear twice as large, while the darkness of night rendered a fairy-tale view of rolling hillside invisible beyond.

Upon further inspection, only the rose-shaped tea lights ensconced in crystal holders at the center of each table were actually wax; flickering, flame-shaped bulbs in every other fixture negated the daunting task that would have been required to keep each one lit with real candles.

Smooth stone walls curled upward toward a dome of glass and iron, wrought in a filigree pattern and punctuated by more roses carved from marble. Truly stunning, the skylight served as a fitting topper to the opulent, multi-level room below. Kitchen staff moved deftly in and out of two swinging doors situated unobtrusively at one end of the hall. In order to get to guests seated near the elevated stage at the far end of the room, waiters were forced to arc around the sunken dance floor dominating the center. At this late hour, the kitchen was still serving dinner, but since most everyone had already cleared their plates, many couples twirled and swayed elegantly across the space. In another hour, the menu would be switching over to gourmet pub fare. If memory served, their duck fat fries with truffles were well worth the wait.

Chloe searched for Lila among the tables while the others stared, slack-jawed at the sight; she wasn't immune to the magical scene spread before her, but since she had been here several times before, Chloe's eyes were more capable of piercing through the crowd than anyone else's.

Eventually, Chloe spotted her mother in the farthest, quietest corner of the room. Lila, dressed to the nines, leaned toward an unquestionably handsome man who grasped her dainty hand in his, Heads together, it was a tender moment. Chloe took the opportunity to observe the body language between the pair, before moving to join them at an intimate table tucked against the windowed wall. Lila was clearly smitten; that much Chloe already knew, so she brushed the thought aside and instead focused on Javier's response to her mother's gentle touches and sparkling-eyed glances.

From this vantage point, with the two completely unaware they were being watched—and also judged—Chloe would have been willing to bet Javier returned Lila's love in kind. His awed smile conveyed an underlying incredulity at his good fortune; he was clearly dazzled, and it wasn't hard to understand why. Lila was a blond flame, scorching nearly every man who had attempted to get close to her since Chloe's father's unfortunate passing more than thirty years before. Perhaps she was finally sated; Chloe took a certain amount of comfort at the thought.

"Over here," she guided EV and Nate toward Lila's table. When Lila turned her head and noticed them coming, Chloe tossed her a jaunty wave.

"Welcome, my loves." Lila drawled, kissing Chloe, EV, and Nate on each cheek in turn, then ushering them toward Javier for another round of niceties. "This is Javier, my *fiancé*." Her tongue rolled over the word.

Chloe whirled to face Javier, taking in his deep, tawny skin, soft eyes the color of tanned leather, and perfectly symmetrical nose up close for the first time. For once, Lila had picked a man closer to her own age, but who, like herself, looked at least a decade younger. Perhaps it was a leisurely lifestyle that stalled the ravages of age, or maybe just good genes. Either way, Javier's appearance was the perfect yin to Lila's yang.

He rose to greet the new arrivals with a warm smile and a handshake. Chloe was glad he hadn't gone for the awkward cheek kissing thing—or worse, a back of the hand kiss.

"I'm so happy to meet all of you." His voice was smooth, with only the hint of an accent, which meant he'd probably spent a lot of time away from home. "Lila has told me many stories of her family and friends. Forgive me if this sounds rude, Chloe, but I feel like we are already family."

Turning to Lila with an arched brow, Chloe made the dry comment, "She wasn't quite as forthcoming with stories about you." She turned back to

Javier, "Tell me about yourself." The words had the flavor of a dare; just the slightest confrontational edge.

Nate nudged her ankle under the table.

Before Chloe had a chance to push, EV said, "Lila tells us you work for a security company. That sounds like an interesting field. Do you do primarily residential or commercial work?" Reading Chloe's aggression as protectiveness, she thought establishing Javier's financial credentials might ease the notion that he was after Lila's money. He wouldn't have been the first man to find that aspect of her worth pursuing.

Answering for him, Lila said, "Javi owns Garritek."

"I've heard of them. Excellent reputation," Nate's eyes went unfocused for a minute while he pinned down the particulars in his mind. "Global tech company. No defense contracts, but big in the private sector." He shot Javier a raised eyebrow, "You guys work with some serious tech." His tone was a high-five of admiration.

"We've done well over the years." Javier downplayed his success in a self-deprecating way.

Not a pauper, then. Chloe thought. With that

worry off her back, she determined to relax and try to enjoy the meal.

"Tell us how the two of you met." EV said.

Lila and Javier exchanged besotted grins.

"It's a funny story." Lila began. "You know that little bakery we love in St. Tropez, Chlo? L'amie du Pain? Well, I got an early morning craving, so I walked over from the flat I was renting, and on the way back I got my heel caught between two cobblestones."

"I found her there, cursing fluently in four different languages. What a sight; clutching a giant purse in one hand, and a boule in the other, this vision of golden beauty in two-inch heels at six o'clock in the morning. Her shoe, it was stuck fast, and not a hand did she have to aid herself. I did the gallant thing, and set her free."

"One inch heels, love. Barely higher than flats. And you laughed at me first." Her indulgent smile drew a shrug from his shoulders.

"I laughed only at my good fortune. It isn't every day a humble man like me finds his goddess stuck to a street."

Just as Chloe began to think she could like the man, everything changed, and she wondered whether she had relaxed a little too soon. Unless her highly-honed investigative reporting skills had deteriorated, there was something off about him. Once talk turned to how many people were free to attend the wedding on such short notice, this close to the start of the holiday season—and to his family in particular—Javier's countenance turned guarded. Nearly every family-related question he passed off with an agility that Chloe felt could have only been developed with considerable practice.

"So, Javier, tell us about your family. Are they able to attend the wedding?" Chloe prodded, a skeptical edge to her voice that prompted a scathing look from Lila and bewildered expressions from both Nate and EV. She ignored a kick in the shins from beneath the table and waited patiently for Javier's response.

Javier slowly finished chewing before answering vaguely, "Many of them will attend, yes. But they won't arrive until just before the ceremony."

Lila interrupted before Javier could say much more. "Javier's sister-in-law, Baylee, is here already; they're very close. Actually, she's an amazing photographer and has graciously agreed to shoot the wedding. When you see her portfolio you'll understand why we accepted, even though there's a perfectly competent photographer on staff here at the castle."

As Chloe opened her mouth to ask another intrusive question, their dinner was interrupted by Antoine, who asked to speak to Javier in private.

"Please excuse me while I attend to some business." He kissed Lila on the cheek before departing.

"What was that all about?" Chloe demanded, suspicion evident in her clipped tone.

Lila sighed. "Back off, Chlo. Javier just told you he's in security. His company oversaw the installation of a high-tech system here about six months ago, and agreed to perform a security scan during our stay. In exchange, they've comped all our suites. Not that we can't afford it, but the wedding rates here are pricey, and we were happy to accept the rate reduction. Besides, it will keep him occupied while we attend to wedding plans."

Wanting clarification, she pressed, but Lila adeptly sidestepped Chloe's onslaught of questions; waxing on about her dress, the ceremony, and the minutiae of other details necessary to pull off an event of this magnitude on such short notice.

Until she changed the subject altogether with a startling question: "Not to be blunt, but what are your intentions toward my daughter?" Lila turned a gimlet-eyed stare toward Nate.

"Did we just time travel back to the dark ages? Who asks that kind of question?" Chloe ignored the snort EV hastily covered by clearing her throat. The woman had been extraordinarily quiet all evening long.

"It's fine," Nate laid a hand over Chloe's to calm her down. "I love her. I've always loved her, and my intentions are to keep on loving her. Will that do it for you?"

Thankfully, Javier returned just in time to put an end to that discussion. He'd barely seated himself when dessert was served.

"Is anything wrong, Dear?"

"I apologize; a guest reported something stolen from her room. It's all been taken care of." With the subject of family no longer taking center stage, he was back to his effusive self.

Conversation centered around the trivial, until the last delicious morsel was scraped off the last delicate plate.

"I think it's time to turn in. EV is almost asleep at the table. Remember, we've got a busy day tomorrow, ladies. I hope you're not opposed to dinner for breakfast. Our tasting with catering starts right here at 9:00 am sharp. I'll see you then." Lila pulled Chloe close for one last, clingy hug before leaving the table with Javier's protective hand at her back.

"All right, sourpuss, what's your deal?" EV demanded when the coast was clear. Nothing about Javier had set off any alarm bells with her.

Nate nodded in agreement. "He seems nice enough. A little nervous about his family, but you're not exactly making it easy on the guy, are you?"

"I know when something is off, and there's definitely something wonky going on with him. And I'd appreciate it if you'd both climb off of my butt. I have every right to scrutinize. It's not like she isn't watching you and me like a hawk. You think she would hesitate to grill you like a steak if she hadn't seen you in diapers?" came Chloe's irritated retort. "Trust me, she's trying to figure out our relationship just as much as I'm trying to figure out theirs. Why do you think she stuck you in a room as far away as she could find? She wants to catch us sneaking into each other's beds. She probably gotten Mr. Security to set up some kind of alarm on my room."

"All the same, let's just put a pin in it for now. You've been dead set against Javier from the second

Lila mentioned she was seeing someone seriously. Do you doubt that we are also good judges of character?"

Chloe crossed her arms and refused to respond. EV hoped a good night's sleep would calm her friend's nerves. "I'll let you two say goodnight. I'm heading to bed. 9:00 am, remember?"

Chapter 5

The restaurant dining room looked entirely different in the harsh light of morning. Empty of guests—other than the three women ensconced at a table dressed with flawless white linen—the vast space echoed with quiet. Breakfast was served in another banquet room, buffet-style. As always, a team of servers and attendants milled around wherever Lila went, some more obtrusively than others.

Even Antoine, whose list of responsibilities bordered on myriad status, skulked nearby whenever he had the time. The only person in the group who dared give Lila the side-eye was the wedding planner employed by the management whom Lila had cut out of the proceedings with surgical precision. Brides often brought in outside help, but rarely planned their own nuptials. Lila's insistence on doing so was a slap in the face.

Considering the speed with which she was putting this whole thing together, Chloe was amazed to see no trace of impatience or stress in her mother's behavior. She simply moved from one laborious task to the next, confident in her decisions down to the most minute detail.

Who are you, and what have you done with my mother? If proximity to Javier brought out this calm and collected persona, Chloe might have to change her mind about him. Clearly, he'd found some way to soothe the beast—something no one else had ever come close to doing. Chloe considered the idea, briefly. *On second thought, it can't last.* Maybe she should start up a bet with EV over how long it would take for Lila to melt down.

One of the impeccably starched and pressed waiters delivered a platter of appetizer options to the center of the table with a flourish. EV reached for a mini tart that looked like a quiche, but turned out to be filled with goat cheese and zucchini. Not exactly breakfast fare, it was, nevertheless, delicious.

"Try one of these," she handed one to Chloe, who rolled her eyes heavenward in appreciation at the first bite.

"Yum. Mom, you have to serve these. They're amazing."

Lila tasted, hummed with pleasure, and made a note on the pad provided her by the chef.

Fifteen bites later, the appetizer menu expanded to include pan seared steak in lettuce cups; toasted brioche with creme fraiche and caviar; bacon-wrapped oysters; and crostini with a variety of toppings. It took another hour to sample their way through all of the entree and side options.

Some quick, albeit approximate, math told Chloe this much food would feed far more people than were expected to attend the wedding.

"Mom, the entire castle staff is going to be taking home leftovers if you order all that. How many people did you say RSVP'd?"

Lila stared blankly at Chloe for a moment before responding. "What difference does that make, Dear? We want people to have choices, don't we? After all, our guests are coming from all over the world." She tilted her head slightly to one side, the gesture a mimic of Chloe's own expression. "Oh, for crying out...Antoine? Come here a moment!" The little man nearly hopped over a table in his haste to do Lila's bidding. "Can you ensure that the leftover food from the wedding will get eaten by someone, and not thrown away?"

"Of course, Miss Lila—" He was cut short by Lila's impatient sigh, and without another glance at the simpering man, she turned back to Chloe.

"Happy, daughter of mine?" Lila's raised right eyebrow indicated that anything other than confirmation would not be tolerated.

"Fine, fine, do whatever you want. Your guests' high cholesterol is all on you, though. Speaking of— when we're done here, I'd say we'd all better hit the gym." Chloe rubbed her stomach and stifled a yawn.

"After this, we're going to choose place settings and party favors," Lila reminded, exasperation filling her voice at her daughter's obvious unfamiliarity with the itinerary she had emailed to Chloe and EV just this morning. "Cake tasting tomorrow. Ring any bells?"

"And a partridge in a pear tree..." Chloe sung under her breath, just loud enough to force a poorly-stifled giggle from EV.After a day spent in the backwash of Lila's wake as she barreled through her list, EV thought if she saw one more china pattern—and for the love of tiny pickles, what difference did it make if the edge pattern on one white-on-white plate was a quarter inch wider than another—she might just toss something. Maybe her cookies, or maybe the china. Or maybe Lila herself.

Several times during the day, her phone had signaled incoming texts. Each time she pulled it out to check, Lila ordered her to put it away. To keep peace, she humored the bride-to-be, but not without a silent, narrow-eyed look of protest.

Owing to a town-wide commitment to honor any and all forms of religious and secular observations, Ponderosa Pines put on a Yule celebration incorporating a diversity of symbols—without rhyme, reason, or the least nod toward political correctness. Santa and his sleigh topping the manger scene was probably the least offensive mixing of traditions, but their hearts were in the right place, and it was all meant in the spirit of love and acceptance.

Now that she finally had a minute to look, she found a series of texts from Allegra. Expecting multiple requests for putting out fires, EV was pleasantly surprised to see images and terse descriptions of everything moving along exactly as laid out in her notes. With a low whistle, she called Chloe over to check it out.

"Allegra's got the Yule under control, take a look."

"Is that Lottie setting up Rudolph? Check out the look on her face. She's not happy."

"There's an email here from her as well," EV grinned. "It's a very restrained tirade. I've decided not to respond." She did, however, shoot off a missive complimenting Allegra on her organizational skills. The woman had untapped depths, of that EV was now certain.

Spread like a deflated balloon over a lounge chair, EV never even twitched when Chloe settled into the adjacent seat with a sigh. Though the winter air here was warmer than Ponderosa Pines at this time of year, EV had draped a blanket over herself while relishing the crisp, clean air.

Several minutes passed before Chloe spoke into the silence, "I never thought it was possible to dread seeing another bite of cake."

EV groaned. "Five cake flavors, seven types of icing. That's thirty-five different combinations. Thirty-five. By the end of it, I couldn't tell the difference. I think I'm suffering sugar shock."

"It was all I could do to keep from screaming, *just pick one.*"

"But not the rum cake." They said it in unison then laughed at themselves for thinking alike.

"I actually think I'm a little buzzed from it." Chloe said. "I'm surprised it didn't slosh onto the plate."

"And what about the one with the raspberry preserves between the layers? With that much rum in the cake, it tasted like cough syrup." A shudder ran though EV. "Your mother is certifiable."

"Could you believe the way she acted toward that poor florist? I had just been thinking how I hadn't seen her blow up yet, and then...BOOM!" The first glimmer of Bridezilla-type behavior out of Lila had slipped through when the castle's resident florist crashed the cake tasting by wheeling in a cart of fresh-cut flowers heavily laden with scent.

"She really ripped that lady a new one. As if a florist doesn't understand that strong odors affect taste buds!" Lila's condescending tone had driven the woman to tears, and only softened infinitesimally when it became clear that Lila herself had double-booked the two appointments.

Through the open balcony doors, they heard the shrill sound of the phone in their suite ringing.

"You get it, it's probably your mother wanting us to taste forty different kinds of candy for the wedding favors." Just thinking about it made EV feel nauseated.

"You get it, then. I can't say no to her; you'll have to do it."

"We could just ignore it," EV suggested.

"No! If we don't answer, she'll just show up here and drag us back to wedding hell."

Not wanting to face that option right now, EV levered herself off the chair to go pick up the phone.

"Hello?"

"Miss Torrence, I have a gentleman here who insists he must speak with you immediately. Please hold the line."

She hardly had time to run through the possibilities before Dalton's voice rang in her ear. "EV, I had to come."

Her pulse sped up; maybe from the edge of anxiety in his voice, but mostly from knowing he was here.

"What's happened? Is something wrong back home?"

"No, it's not that. Bring Chloe and come down here. Nate's already on his way." He hung up in her ear without providing any more info.

Pitching her voice to be heard on the balcony, EV said, "haul your lazy butt in here." Given the urgency in her voice, Chloe wasted no time.

"What's going on?"

"That was Dalton. He's here."

Chloe's mouth dropped open. "He's here? Oh, that's so sweet. He couldn't stand to be without you." EV did an internal double-take as Chloe, ever-suspicious and generally skeptical, jumped to the most romantic of conclusions.

Could that have been part of his decision to come? A little flare of satisfaction washed over EV at the thought, yet she maintained an even, dry tone when she said, "He asked for you and Nate on his way downstairs as well, so I'm thinking he had another motive for flying halfway around the world."

"That's a load of bull, and you know it. If there was a break in the case, he could have picked up the phone. If he's here, he's here for you," Chloe smirked.

EV scrunched her face into an exaggeration of Chloe's smirk, "Let's go find out."

Nate beat them to the lobby by a good five minutes. His banishment to the farthest possible spot from Chloe's suite put him on a more direct route to the front desk. Once there, he helped Dalton sort out the problem of not having a reservation when every room would be booked for the wedding. Antoine stepped in, swapping them to a larger suite with a second bedroom. Someone else would get bumped to a smaller room, but Antoine assured Nate he would make it work.

So much for Chloe embarking on any late night visits. He watched her walk down the stairs toward him and, even now, knowing only something major would drag Dalton here so quickly, all he could think about was kissing the breath out of his beautiful girlfriend. He did his best to banish the thought, at least for the time being.

"What's going on?" Chloe demanded.

"Not here," Nate hissed. "We'll talk about it upstairs." He pocketed the new room keys Antoine handed him, and led the way.

The door opened into a shared seating area of sorts. A pair of sofas in subdued, cream-colored upholstery flanked a black lacquered coffee table. Beyond them, a four-seater table sat in front of the stationary half of a sliding door leading to a balcony. Unlike EV and Chloe's room, there was no kitchenette. Just a pair of bedroom doors opposite each other at the far end of the room. On the right, a coat closet took up the space behind the door, and on the left was a small, but elegantly appointed bathroom.

Stepping into the cozy suite, EV sensed undercurrents of strong emotion. She took in Dalton's ramrod-straight back, tense shoulders, and clenched fists, along with Nate's flat-eyed cop face, and jumped to the most obvious conclusion.

"Remy's coming to the wedding." Nothing else would have caused Dalton to leave Ponderosa Pines unprotected. Not that the job was enough to occupy anyone on a full-time basis; should anything happen, Gilmore PD was one quick phone call away. No, EV knew something else had brought him here. Despite their agreement to put their relationship on hold while dealing with Remy, he would have come in the first place, if she had asked.

"According to Marjorie." Dalton deadpanned, his haggard face matched a voice clogged with fatigue. In the past twenty-four hours, he'd managed to spend only a scant three in sleep on the plane. Turbulence and the intense desire to protect EV from having to face Remy alone brought him alert far too often for the nap to be considered restful. Now, his eyes drank her in, while also searching for signs that this new development was too painful for her to bear.

EV went silent for a moment while she flipped through an internal catalog of her own emotions. Anxiety over having to face her ex again after all this time—check. Dread of having to tell Lila the whole sordid tale of her past—check. Worse, having to possibly hash that out with Remy—check. And finally, a deeply-seated satisfaction over playing avenging angel for her town—big fat check.

That last didn't exactly cancel out the rest, but cushioned them enough to spread a savage grin over her face. "What's the plan? Whatever you need me to do, I'm in."

"If I've never said it before," Dalton walked over and kissed her soundly on the lips. "You're one hell of a woman, Emmalina Torrence."

Chloe, delighted at seeing the kiss, let out a loud *whoop* that forced Nate to crack a smile. With the tension released, Chloe ordered a couple of pizzas from room service—hoping to counteract the threatening sugar coma—and the four of them sat down at the table to hammer out a plan for getting to the bottom of Remy's vendetta against Ponderosa Pines.

"I could see him coming back to take some sort of revenge against me, though for what reason, I have no idea. But what could he have against an entire town?" EV frowned. "And more importantly, why now? He's been nothing but a bad memory for thirty years. Something must have triggered him. And Marjorie still has no clue? I don't get it."

"That's been the problem all along. Without a clear motive, we're struggling to make what evidence we do have fit any kind of actionable reason for what he seems to be trying to accomplish. Best we've got now is several counts of identity theft." Nate snagged the last piece of pizza. "Even if he'd managed to get Evan to convince the town to throw in the towel and combine with Gilmore, I can't see any profit in it for him. He has no financial stake in Gilmore that I can find. They've been very helpful over there, by the way. Not just the police department; the entire town management team."

His comment pulled a raised eyebrow from EV. In her experience, the leaders of the town of Gilmore had always looked down on the residents of Ponderosa Pines. It was easy to forget the fact that Nate had been top dog back in Portland; his foray as a small-town lawman seemed natural to her, but perhaps his status legitimized Ponderosa Pines in the eyes of Gilmore's officials.

Dalton took up the narrative. "Nate's investigator friend dropped off everything she's found so far." He twisted in his chair to grab the briefcase he'd brought with him, and pulled out a sheaf of papers.

Jumping up to clear the pizza leavings from the table, Chloe brushed past Nate. The momentary touch raised goosebumps on her arms, and for a second she considered kicking Dalton out of his own room. *Love ya, Dalton, but you're blocking me pretty hard right now.* Just as Veronica and Mindy had suggested, it looked like skulking around the castle for some alone time was their only option.

As Dalton laid out the papers, EV snatched each one up, scanned it quickly, then placed it back on the table. What she saw was enough for her to know Remy was the culprit. There was even enough evidence that Nate had been given the green light to officially reopen the investigation, but no judge would issue a warrant based on what they had amassed so far.

An hour later, Dalton's eyes were drooping and the bones of a plan had formed.

Chapter 6

Chloe's usually-groomed hair fell in a disordered mess around her face—the result of running her hands through it while resisting the urge to yank it out by the roots. Listening to Lila argue with the sacrificial lamb of a liaison to the atrium manager over why it wasn't prudent to unleash five hundred live butterflies indoors was right up there with getting her teeth cleaned on Chloe's list of least favorite things to do. That the seemingly timid little mouse had drawn the short straw was evident. Remarkably, she held her ground and insisted Lila have the wedding of her dreams, while remaining within managerial guidelines. EV had been alternating between silent laughter and slipping into some state of meditative avoidance ever since Lila's dainty hands hammered on the connecting door right before she let herself into Chloe's room earlier that morning.

With caffeine coursing through her system, Chloe could handle her mother in full-on diva mode, but before breakfast, she was a little much to take.

"Butterflies do not poop." Lila's near shriek knocked the zen right off of EV, who beat a hasty retreat to the bathroom. Seeing EV's lips pressed tightly together, Chloe suspected it was to keep from peeing her pants with laughter.

Traitor, Chloe's eyes shot daggers at EV's back before she gave in to the inevitable and stepped into the fray. She waived the harried young woman—whose only error had been trying to placate the bride beast—out the door before rounding on Lila.

"*Everything* poops, Mother. Give it a rest. It's not going to happen. Don't we need to be somewhere else right now?" Sighing, Chloe pressed fingers to her temple; the ache there was starting to throb.

Lila glanced at her watch. "Yes, we need to meet Baylee in the café in five minutes." She pitched her voice louder, "Get out here, EV, we're leaving now."

Before Lila could pull open the door, a loud knocking preceded the shrill, singsong question, "Where's my newest bri-ide? Are you in there Lila?" A pause. "Hellooo." Whoever was on the other side of the door had the voice of a whining child; her tone pierced the air like the screech of metal on metal.

"Shh." Whispering, Lila said, "Be quiet and maybe she'll go away."

"Who is it?" When one person whispers, everyone does. Chloe nudged Lila aside to squint through the peephole. It could have been the distortion from the fish eye lens, but the woman on the other side of the door reminded Chloe of the Cabbage Patch Doll she'd bugged her mother for when she was little. Blond hair framed a round, dimpled face with a button nose. Chloe had to stand on tiptoes and angle her gaze downward in order to see the tiny woman.

"Hush up, she'll hear you. That's Hannah Frank, former wedding coordinator to the stars."

"Former?" EV also whispered.

"Lot of rumors. Some kind of scandal put her out of commission. Now she's trying to work her way back in. She heard I was getting married and followed me here."

Chloe watched Hannah frown, then reluctantly walk away. "She's gone. And now that you mention it, I received an alert from one of my social media monitoring tools that your name was tweeted—the post came from *HF Events*, and mentioned your engagement. I figured it was legit; that maybe you had hired a wedding planner, so I didn't think much of it at the time."

"What does she want?" EV asked.

"To help with the wedding. Gratis, of course, because she just happened to be staying at the castle. Coincidence? I doubt it." Why was she still whispering? "I think she's trying to use me to get back in good graces with her former clientele." Lila added in her normal tone of voice. "I told her we're planning a small, understated wedding and I don't need her help. Apparently, I wasn't speaking her language."

"I see." EV grinned. "A small, understated wedding. In a castle, with 500 butterflies, and how many of your closest friends?"

"Hey, I'm only going to do this once." Lila answered EV's grin with one of her own. "But I don't want that twin-set-wearing airhead involved."

"So, just tell her that." Chloe suggested.

"You make it sound so easy. I'll tell you what," Lila retorted, "You try it when she comes around again. See how far you get. She's more relentless than a bulldog. I already had to warn the staff not to take orders from her after I found out she'd been telling everyone she was in charge. I caught Antoine just before he sent back the four racks of bridesmaids dresses I ordered in from various sources. He had no idea she wasn't legit. I think that's why his nose is so brown right now; he's feeling guilty."

"The nerve."

"I think she's gone. We're going to be late for our lunch with the photographer." Lila hoped Hannah wasn't lurking around the next corner. While EV and Chloe exchanged amused sidelong glances, Lila sidled along the wall and peeked around just to make sure.

"Clear."

When Lila glanced back, it was to see EV and Chloe doing their best Charlie's Angels imitation. Lila looked away to hide her grin, and maybe, even if she would never admit it, her jealousy that the two of them were so close. A visit to Ponderosa Pines might not be the worst thing. After saying she would consider one to attend EV's wedding to Dalton when she thought such a thing impossible, Lila now hoped it would come to pass.

Baylee Delarosa and her assistant Ross Adams were already seated at one of the larger tables in the café's atrium when Lila breezed in with her entourage—if Chloe and EV could be called that. After kissing Baylee on both cheeks and offering an apology for her tardiness, Lila made the introductions.

Running an appraising eye over the attractive woman who stood waiting to shake her hand, Chloe judged Baylee to be in her early forties. A swing of smooth auburn hair framed an oval face scattered across the middle with freckles. A ready smile bracketed by the kind of fine creases that came from long years of practice contradicted the shallower frown lines etching their way into her forehead. The soft twang in her speech pattern gave away a childhood spent in Georgia before moving to Europe after college.

"Baylee is married to Javier's brother, Tomas." Lila explained when everyone was seated once more. "We're going to be sisters-in-law."

"Congratulations." The shadow that flickered through Baylee's eyes was gone so quickly Chloe later decided she had imagined it.

Leaning sideways in her seat, Baylee looked toward the entrance. "Isn't Javier coming?"

Lila sighed, "No. He's somewhere in the bowels of the castle talking shop with the security techs about the updates and resets or whatever it is he has to do while we are here."

"That's our Javi, always on the job."

"Even when he's on vacation." Lila smiled indulgently. "I'm sure he'll have it sorted out in no time."

Ross, a strapping young lad of no more than twenty, couldn't manage to keep his dark eyes focused on the conversation, given the way a pair of similarly-aged young women not-so-subtly flirting with him from their table at the other end of the room. "Now that you've met Lila and her family, I think it's okay if you go take some personal time." He lingered only long enough to toss a *nice meeting you* in their general direction before sauntering over to chat up his admirers.

"Oh, to be young and hormonal." EV mocked with good humor.

"I'm fine with being old and hormonal." Lila waggled her eyebrows suggestively.

"Can we please change the subject? I'm getting mental images, and there's no such thing as brain bleach." Chloe complained.

For the next few minutes, while Chloe fidgeted and EV's eyes glazed over, Lila chatted with Baylee about things that had more to do with her soon-to-be family than with the real purpose for this luncheon. When she could take no more, Chloe cleared her throat, "Have you had a lot of experience with wedding photography?" The question sounded abrupt, though she hadn't meant it that way.

"Would you like to see my portfolio? Your mother tells me you've done some work in the industry as well." While she spoke, Baylee pulled an iPad from her bag, cuing it up to start a slideshow.

"Mostly fashion. A couple weddings." Chloe answered absently, her attention focused on the play of images across the small screen.

"Lovely." EV ventured, after watching Chloe flick through fifteen or so images.

"You have a great eye for color, and a knack for

catching those candid moments that tell a story." Chloe couldn't help but admire the skill. "These are spectacular."

"Thank you." Baylee said sincerely.

"There's one thing, though." Lila said. "Well, two, really. First, make sure to catch my best side; and second, you're also a guest at this wedding, so I hope you'll take some time out for a little fun." Chloe heard lightheartedness and also something weightier, more serious, in Lila's command.

"And Photoshop out all my wrinkles." EV chimed in. "And the zit that's going to pop up on Chloe's forehead six hours before the shindig."

"Seriously? Thanks for cursing me, evil one." Chloe tossed an exaggerated mock glare at EV. "If it happens, there will be payback."

"I'd expect nothing less." EV looked at Lila. "Did she tell you what she did to me with the online dating service?"

"You started it."

"Now, now, children." Lila cautioned. Baylee listened and laughed with the three animated women who were going to be a joy to photograph.

Half an hour later, amid empty plates, Lila put both elbows on the table and leaned forward to say conspiratorially, "If a troll named Hannah tells you she's my wedding coordinator, you ignore her and call me right away. The woman is delusional, and I wouldn't let her coordinate my dog's birthday party."

"Hannah Frank? I've heard of her before." Baylee's tone suggested none of what she had heard was good, "Wasn't she involved in some sort of fracas last year?" Baylee searched her mind. "The details were kept hush-hush, which probably makes it sound worse than it was."

"That's the one. Just keep an eye out for her, and ignore anything she tells you to do." Lila tapped her fingers on the table.

"You should be able to pick her out of the crowd pretty easily, she's a cross between Barbie and Hitler." An inelegant snort almost caused Baylee's drink to fly out of her mouth at EV's dry comment.

Chapter 8

As chance would have it, EV, taking advantage of a break in wedding detail duty, had decided to check out the gym, and was walking past the reception area when a familiar voice cut through the air like a knife. Every muscle in her body tensed.

"I told you, I don't have a reservation, but you must have a suite available. It's common practice to keep one open in case a VIP shows up. I'm here for a wedding." EV could almost hear his eyes rolling in their sockets. "Lila LaRue's wedding."

Whatever murmured words Antoine's counterpart behind the desk said, EV couldn't hear, but the tone of them implied that Remy Vincent was not very important. To keep him from seeing her before she was ready to deal with him, EV ducked out of sight behind a fluted column just a second too late. The castle cat caught sight of his new favorite human and padded over. EV waved him away. The cat thoroughly ignored her efforts. Reaching down, EV lifted him into her arms where, purring loudly, he settled in. His presence gave EV a measure of comfort while she waited for events to unfold.

She listened to the five-minute argument that ensued before he was finally offered a room he considered adequate. The condescending way he spoke to the hotel employee mimicked the tone he'd used with her during their last few weeks together. Time split into *then* and *now*. Her body wanted to cower; to respond to the ancient *then*, and slink away from its icy embrace. Two deep breaths wheezed through her before a sob tried to escape. EV clenched her fists, nails digging scarlet crescents into her palms. The pinch of physical pain cleared her head. She willed her shoulders to loosen from the bonds of tension gathered there.

That one conscious act triggered another—her jaw slackened; teeth aching from being ground together separated; the knot in her stomach slithered, unwound. A calm settled over her like a shower of warm spring rain. *The past only has power over you if you choose to grasp it tightly. Only by letting go can you remain anchored in the present.*

Now pushed *then* off a cliff to dash upon the rocks of *never again*. *Now* was all that was left. *Now* she was free. EV ran up the stairs in a weightless rush.

She found Chloe and Nate on the couch, fused together like teenagers.

"Get a room." Her voice startled the two of them apart.

"This is my room." Frustration painted a sharp, stony edge on the words until Chloe got a good look at EV's face. Something was different. It was subtle, but Chloe knew everything had changed. "What happened?" She sat up, breaking away from Nate, and leaned forward to hear.

EV slumped onto the nearly love seat-sized chair opposite the sofa. "Remy just checked in."

Instantly, Chloe's body tensed as she went on full alert. "Did you talk to him? Did he see you? Tell me."

"No and no. I saw him, but he didn't see me. I hid behind a column and listened to him act like a total asshat to the staff. He browbeat his way into a suite in the south wing."

"That's over near the end of the castle that hasn't been fully renovated yet. It's worse than the area Mom stuck Nate in." Concern tilted Chloe's head; she gave EV the once over to gauge her mood. What she saw settled the matter. Rock solid hands, relaxed shoulders, and a sense of calm. "You're not freaked out." Chloe jumped up to do a little booty-shaking victory dance. "Not even a little."

"No, I'm..."

Before EV finished the thought, Dalton burst through the door. The second EV mentioned Remy's name, Nate had grabbed his phone to shoot off a 911 text. Dalton must have been on his way there already to have gotten to the room so quickly.

He went straight to EV pulled her to her feet, and then rested hands on her shoulders. "Are you okay?" The question was purposefully vague, because Dalton couldn't ask the one he really wanted answered, which was: *do you still have feelings for him?*

Almost giddy with relief from the emotional baggage she'd dropped behind that column, EV nearly sang, "I'm fine—better than fine, actually. He's going down, right?" She asked, plunking onto a chintz armchair.

It was Dalton's turn to feel relieved. "Oh, yeah all the way." He nudged EV over, slid into the chair beside her, and grabbed her hand for a quick squeeze before turning his attention to Nate. "What's his next move? And how do we plan to counter it?"

"I'm betting he'll start by contacting Lila—see what she has to say; get the lay of the land. Then, he'll move on to setting up a chance meeting with EV. He'll want an audience, so I'm thinking he'll sweep in during dinner, lock eyes across the room. Fake surprise. Give her the old *we really should catch up, let's get together to talk about old times* routine. I can't imagine him coming up with anything more original than that."

"He'll be watching you closely to see your reaction. Do you think you can handle it? Be honest—and if you can't, we'll figure out another way." Chloe's first concern was for EV.

"Oh no. I'm fine. Trust me—*he's* been out of my head for years; today just confirmed that fact. I'm all over it."

"Okay, good. You two brainstorm." Chloe waved a hand to indicate Nate and Dalton. "We're going to go polish up the bait."

Chloe laughed at the confused look on EV's face. "Spa day, hit the salon, get you all dolled up. You'll feel more confident when he gets a look at you and turns into a drooling idiot." She laughed again when EV's face fell. "Good grief, it's not like I'm dragging you off to the torture chamber. It's a mani-pedi and a facial. Come on. When was the last time you let anyone pamper you? Probably never. I'll be right there with you, and we'll charge the whole thing off to Mother's room. She was going to insist, anyway. She's occupied at the moment; let's leave her out of it —trust me, it will be more pleasant this way. You could use a little smoothing of the nerves before we get to the dress-choosing portion of the wedding extravaganza, anyway."

Before EV could utter another word of protest, Chloe had her by the arm and was pulling her out the door.

"You know I hate being fussed over." Dalton heard her say, her voice fading into the distance.

He turned to Nate, "If he hurts her, I'll..."

"We won't let that happen."

"Count on it. He doesn't touch her. Period."

The spa was located—appropriately, EV thought—in the castle's former dungeon. "We don't even have an appointment. There's no way we're getting in."

Chloe tossed her an amused look, "My mother drops a fortune every time she stays here; they'd probably fly a flag with her face on it if she asked them to. Trust me, we'll get the works."

"Wonderful." Sarcasm laced the word with poisonous intent.

"Oh, loosen up a little. It's nice to be pampered once in a while. You might like it."

"See, that's the problem. You act like I've never had a spa day before, and so will they. I'll walk in there, and the minute they get a look at my hands, the head tilting will start."

"The what, now?"

"You know, the sympathetic head tilt. Sometimes they even make that *tsk* noise. Then you can practically see the wheels turning while they try to decide what drastic measures I'll need."

Biting her lip, Chloe tried to stifle a grin and failed. "Bet they ask what you use on your face, though. Whatever Thelma puts in that cream she makes, it is magic. If you used it on your hands, you wouldn't get the tilt-y head faces."

They hit the bottom of the stairs where a pair of thick glass doors whooshed open as if on cue.

"Be nice." Chloe hissed. "And try to enjoy this."

For all her bluster, EV was looking forward to a couple of hours sans tension. Dalton showing up here with Remy practically on his heels put a few knots in her shoulders. Normally, she would have worked the kinks out on the big punching bag hanging in her bedroom. The castle boasted its own gym, just not one fully stocked to her tastes in exercise. Given the choice between running in place or pouring her anxieties into a righteous beating on something, she'd go for the latter.

They stepped inside, where EV watched Chloe greet some of the staff as though it hadn't been at least three years since their last meeting. After a round of cheek kissing, Chloe introduced EV, who got the same treatment.

As Chloe had predicted, schedules were immediately shuffled and EV was dragged into a whirlwind of peace and tranquility wrapped in terrycloth softness. The next three hours passed in a blur of sensations; hot stones, moist facial masks, slippery seaweed wraps, and the coolness of peppermint foot cream.

Every bit of tension had been soothed out of her by the time those glass doors whooshed open again.

The calm feeling lasted only until Chloe's next sentence. "Now for hair and makeup."

"I'd like to submit a formal protest." EV knew it was pointless, but she tried anyway.

"Denied. Come on. It's time you met Patrice."

A second round of cheek kissing ensued while the staff assured Chloe she was putting them to no trouble. Another flurry of activity, and an absolutely stunning woman—wearing unrelieved black and clutching a rat-tailed comb with an end sharp enough to qualify as a weapon—circled her speculatively. A similarly-clad flock of underlings waited, each one poised to take action at their leader's command.

Shock-white hair angled from the nape of Patrice's neck to curve around blade-sharp cheekbones set high above a narrow chin. A fringe of white cut a line above sea green eyes that took in every detail of EV's appearance.

Mild panic set in when Patrice reached out to sift a lock of sable strands through her fingers.

"Virgin." she pronounced in a heavy French accent. "It is rare—unprocessed hair. Good color. You cut it yourself, no?"

"Well, I..."

"Do not lie. Patrice always knows."

From behind her, EV heard a snicker and knew it

was Chloe. She squared her shoulders. "Yes, I cut it myself." Was this a trip to the Principal's office, or a hairdresser?

"This you must not do." Patrice circled a third time. "Shape is wrong. Those eyes, those cheekbones, you do them no favors." She reversed, circling once more in the opposite direction. "Yes. I will fix." Patrice clapped twice, sending her minions scurrying to do her unspoken bidding, while EV turned to burn Chloe with the force of her glare. Somehow, Chloe managed to keep a straight face while she nodded encouragement, but the second EV turned away again, she pressed her lips together to keep from laughing.

If fear of what Patrice planned to do to her hadn't set EV on edge, she might have enjoyed the shampoo more. As it was, she suspected the beautiful young man who danced expert fingers over her scalp only wore those tight black pants to distract patrons from what lay ahead. It almost worked, too.

When tight-pants finished, he led EV to where Patrice waited next to the Chair of Doom. Even Chloe's head swiveled to watch him leave the room.

Perfectly sculpted though they were, his buns were the last thing on EV's mind as Patrice spun the chair away from the mirror and brandished her pointy-ended comb. The first snick of the scissors sounded like a gong, and EV jumped when Patrice commanded, "Relax. Trust me. I always give good hair."

Since it was too late to turn back now, EV decided to give in. While hair slithered to the floor, Patrice said, "There is someone special, no? A man?"

"It's complicated."

"Complicated." Patrice shrugged. "Flimsy social media word, eh? Still, is better than boring." Without looking, she passed off the scissors and comb." A blow dryer slapped her palm with all the gravity of a surgeon being handed a scalpel. Five minutes later, It was over. Patrice spun the chair and EV finally got a look at herself.

"What do you think?" Chloe burst out. "I love it; you look amazing."

EV turned her head from side to side to fully take in the new look. She'd lost at least half the bulk to choppy layers that skimmed her cheekbones and accentuated her eyes. Patrice was a genius—it was polished, yet artfully messy at the same time.

"It's...Wow! Is that really me?"

"You will not cut it yourself again." Patrice ordered.

"I won't let her." Chloe assured. The soft sound of a camera shutter clicked somewhere behind Chloe, and she could have sworn EV's face brightened momentarily, as if illuminated by a quick flash of light. Glancing around, she noticed a few people milling about the waiting area, but nobody paying special attention to their conversation. *Probably just some tourist taking a selfie,* she thought, chalking up the unnerving feeling of being watched to a mere coincidence.

After a final round of cheek kissing, Chloe forced EV out the door.

"Okay, next we'll get you a new outfit, and then we'll have your makeup done."

"Is this your subtle way of telling me I've been letting myself go?"

"No. It's my in-your-face way of telling you that it's okay to try new things. Plus, it's fun to play dress up." Taking time for a serious moment, Chloe added, "Besides, I thought it might help prepare you for what's coming. I know it's going to be tough on you, because there's no way seeing him doesn't dredge up the past. Think of this as putting up your shields."

"Phasers on stun?" EV's lips quirked.

"No darling, phasers on stunning. You're such a nerd, though. I meant like armor for going into battle, but I guess your analogy works, too."

"I'm going to be fine, you know. He no longer has the power to hurt me."

"Then think of this as your reward. Either way, you're getting new clothes, and it's about time, too."

"What's wrong with my clothes? It's not like I buy all of them at New Sage. I go into Portland and spend the big bucks on labels when I feel like it."

"And when would that be? Twice a decade?"

"I hate shopping."

Chloe considered a response, but finding none of sufficient scorn, she dragged EV into her favorite of the two boutiques.

Back in Ponderosa Pines, Lottie Calabrese paused in her perusal of new decorating ideas on Pinterest to open the email from Chloe when it hit her inbox with a ping. "Holy crow, would you look at that," she breathed when the image of EV in her new finery popped onto the screen. Three keystrokes later, the email winged its way forward to her entire list of contacts in town—which included just about everyone.

In Ireland, Chloe timed it at just under two minutes before the image popped up on Facebook—evidence of what happens when a small-town grapevine goes high tech.

Back in the suite, Lila paced across the plush white carpet in measured steps from the balcony doors through the small sitting area to the bathroom door, and then back again. Where were they? She had news—big news—and no one to share it with.

By the time Chloe pushed open the door, Lila was ready to burst.

"Where have you...?" Lila caught sight of EV; her eyebrows lifted, and she let out a low whistle. "I guess I can see where you've been." She waved her hand in a circular motion to indicate EV should do a spin. "You look gorgeous, but I have big news." Dramatic pause. "Remy's here."

When her words did not land with the expected amount of surprise, Lila's face fell. "You already knew?"

Chloe and EV exchanged a look.

"I was passing through the lobby when he arrived."

Against expectation, EV's bald statement must have lacked a certain angst, because Lila frowned at her.

"What?" EV returned the frown. "I told you I got over him a long time ago. You still see us as a pair of dewy-eyed teenagers deep in the throes of first love. You bailed before things turned really ugly." EV stalked over to a padded barstool facing into the suite's galley-style kitchenette. After a few seconds, Lila retorted, "I had a lot of my plate at the time," then joined her while Chloe pulled bottles of water from the fridge.

The subtext running under the conversation was about as subtle as a tornado in a trailer park.

EV had felt abandoned in her time of need, and so had Lila. Chloe was torn between wanting to give them privacy, and an intense desire to hear every tiny detail. Curiosity won out. She settled on the couch behind them and stayed quiet.

"I wish I'd gone ahead and taken that year off from college right after you lost Alexander. Probably would have saved us both a world of trouble." EV said wryly, hating to bring Chloe's late father into the conversation.

EV laid it all out for Lila—how Remy's carefully

constructed facade had developed cracks; how, during the college years, they'd fought bitterly. Finally, EV described the miscarriage, and how, after secretly burying their baby, Remy had walked away without a backward glance.

"This is a lot to take in all at once." Lila drained the bottle of water; she took a deep breath. "I had no idea. Why didn't you tell me?" Tears shimmered on her lashes.

"You had your own tragedy to contend with at the time. I didn't want to add to your grief by sharing mine."

"All this time," the tears spilled over. "I thought... I'm not sure what I thought, but it wasn't nice. You were so distant, and I had this little baby to raise all alone. I was so angry with you for being so detached when I needed you most."

"That's part of why you left Ponderosa Pines, isn't it? I always thought it was just about losing Dad— not being able to face being there without him." From behind them, Chloe voiced her thoughts.

"Saying it out loud would have made it too real." EV admitted. "You know we're two of a kind—always were. Control freaks more stubborn than one of Zellner's prize mules."

"But we still look damn good for our age." EV toasted Lila's observation with her plastic water bottle.

"I've got a confession to make." Lila said.

"Another one? Should I have broken out the wine?" Chloe moved back into the kitchen section to rest her elbows on the counter. She wasn't about to miss whatever was coming next.

"I invited Remy because I thought you needed the closure."

Twin snorts from Chloe and EV put a frown on Lila's face, until Chloe gave her a short explanation for why Dalton had arrived so precipitously.

"There's more. We believe Remy was behind the blackmail attempt on Evan Plunkett. Nate has some evidence, but not enough for a conviction, and we can't figure out his motive. So..."

"So, you're sending EV in as Mata Hari."

"That's the plan."

Amid the quiet hum of dinner conversation, and the tinkling of silverware, EV strolled into La Sirene with an air of casualness that didn't match the flare of ice traveling along her knotted nerves. Perfectly-cooked meats in butter-laden sauces scented the air like caloric sin. None of them held the least appeal to EV at the moment. She'd just found the fatal flaw in their plan.

The broad strokes of the scheme had been to go to the restaurant and talk with Remy. The step that fell in the middle of those two actions was the one giving her trouble. As predicted, Remy had called Lila to announce his arrival in a manner that suggested the success of the entire event had depended upon his being there. He had not, however, brought up the subject of EV at all. That omission had led them to stage this impending fiasco of an impromptu meeting. Arguing that it played right into his hands, EV had been outvoted and summarily dispatched here with the vague instructions to engineer a chance meeting.

Was she supposed to saunter over to where he dined alone and plunk herself down in the opposite chair? Or, maybe she should just stand here in the doorway like a complete idiot until he noticed her.

Looking for a third alternative, EV scoped out the room. Cream-colored linens and stemware polished to a fare-thee-well gleamed under vintage Lalique. Remy's popularity among the staff was evidenced by his less-than-ideal placement between the swinging kitchen door and the short hallway leading to the restrooms just beyond. If he treated his waiter like he had the unfortunate soul at the front desk, he was likely to get a sneeze burger for dinner.

Watching the ballet of waitstaff moving in and out the door gave EV the ghost of an idea. When the waiter with the sour expression pushed the empty desert cart into the kitchen for a restock, she gave it a full two minutes, then slowly began to make her way toward the restroom area. If she timed it right, she could stage a small scene right near Remy's table.

As it was, she had to pick up her pace when she heard the unmistakable sound of wheels and something bumping the back of the door. The next few seconds required a delicate performance. Lining herself up in the aisle between tables, she played a game of dessert cart chicken. When the waiter dodged left to go around her, she slid in the same direction. When he changed course, she pivoted right on cue, putting her body in close proximity with the rolling menace. The waiter's face fell into politely annoyed lines as EV bumped a hip against Remy's table.

The only blip in her plan was that Remy caught

his water glass before it dumped over into his lap. Petty, she admitted, but it would have been fun to douse him. Instead, she had to satisfy herself with watching his expression change as he recognized her.

"I'm so sorry. I didn't mean to...Remy?" She let her eyes widen in surprise, then filled them with false warmth.

He struggled to replace his initial snarl with a warm greeting. She could see how the effort to drop into character cost him. The veneer of politeness had thinned over the years. And so had his hair.

The way his appraising gaze ran over her made EV glad Chloe had insisted on a makeover. Whatever it was that she had hoped to see—maybe the ghost of the boy she knew had once loved her, or a flicker of regret over the loss of his child and the way he had treated her—there was nothing in him worthy of redemption.

"EV, I was hoping I'd run into you. As soon as I heard about the wedding, I knew I couldn't miss getting a glimpse of the man who finally corralled Lila." He stood. "Are you meeting anyone?" When she shook her head, he snapped impatient fingers at the next passing waiter. "Set another place, the lady will be joining me."

The lady would have preferred slapping him. Or kicking him in the danglies.

"You look good, EV. Beautiful."

"Thank you. You look," *older, paunchier, like a rat bastard with pointy teeth who probably smells like the fetid hole he crawled out of,* "distinguished. Tell me, where have you been keeping yourself all these years?"

"Oh, here and there," he evaded, "My grandfather passed on last year. Since then, I've been handling some of his personal business." He reached across the table to lay a hand on hers. "What about you? Lila tells me you moved into your parent's old place."

"I'm comfortable there." With an eloquent shrug she deflected the conversation back to him. "Did you ever get married? Have children?" *Please tell me you never procreated.*

"Come now, it's bad form to talk about exes on a date."

Date? In your dreams, you fungus on the butt of humanity.

He glanced up when a waiter appeared at his side. Keeping his eyes on EV, Remy ordered steak *au poivre* with cognac sauce and fingerling potatoes.

"And the lady will have the same." He flashed her a triumphant smile.

"The lady will have the chicken with garlic," *Lots and lots of garlic—enough to choke a vampire.* She flashed Remy a pointed look, "and leek soup to start, You'll bill both to my room." Alone again, she said, "This is not a date." The tart comment slid right past him, since it didn't fit with the fantasy that he could snap his fingers and have her panting to be with him again.

Could he be a bigger jerk? His ego obviously outweighed his mental faculties if he couldn't read her complete lack of interest in him. EV took a moment to tune him out and think. Part of her thirsted for payback—the part that lived deep in the most primitive recesses of her mind—for the way he had walked away from her grief over their lost child. For the wild mother in her, this was personal. The primal desire to inflict pain had to be tempered with guile and wit if she wanted to learn his motive for going after Ponderosa Pines.

Listening to him now, even with half her brain otherwise occupied, she was coming to realize his reasons for blackmailing Evan might not have been all that complex. Remy reminded her of an attention-seeking child constantly shouting, "Mommy, look at me!"

The leek soup smelled like heaven, but tasted like dust in her mouth. Spoonful followed spoonful while he prattled on about himself. Her bowl lay empty before he seemed to realize she hadn't spoken since taking that first bite.

"You're quiet, EV. I guess your days run together out there in the woods, living the quiet life."

"I manage to fill my time." Hadn't Marjorie told him EV normally spent half the month of February criss-crossing the country speaking about Ponderosa Pines and the environmental innovations used there? She made a note to have someone ask Remy's aunt that very question. "I'm learning to knit."

"How quaint." Remy's sneer lasted only a second before he shoved a huge chunk of steak into his mouth.

I hope you choke.

Forcing her face into a pleasant mask, EV threw out the first morsel of bait. "Well, you know I've felt obligated to stay ever since I practically forced the elders to expand." EV rolled her eyes, let a small sigh of regret slide his way.

"Then get out. They don't need you now." He

reached across the table to lay his hand over hers. She stopped the involuntary flinch of disgust, but just barely. The prickling feeing originating from the point of contact had nothing to do with desire, and everything to do with the skin of her hand wanting to crawl off her bones and slink under the table like a kicked dog.

"It's not that easy. I have ties in the Pines."

"Lila said you were seeing someone." He let his eyes go dark and hungry. "You know I'm the only one for you, right? We're meant to be. It's kismet."

Kismet? Kiss it. Just pucker up.

EV dipped her head, cast her eyes down toward the table—let him think she was overcome with emotion, and not just hiding the scorn that leapt into them.

"I'd give you anything you want," he continued. "Besides, Ponderosa Pines won't be your problem much longer."

"What do you mean by that?"

"Nothing. Dessert?" He changed the subject.

"Thank you, but I have to meet Lila in," she looked at her watch, "ten minutes."

"When can I see you again."

When I can ski in hell.

One elegantly clad shoulder lifted skyward before EV turned and walked away. She felt his eyes on her the whole time. Under his gaze, she forced her feet to take slow, even steps until, without a backward glance, she turned the corner and he could no longer see her. EV slipped off the torturous heels Chloe had made her wear, and lengthened her stride to a fast walk. She welcomed the distance each step put between her and the restaurant.

Replaying the scene back in her head, EV looked for clues she might have missed the first time. A tell-tale eye twitch, a firming of the lips—anything to build on the next time she had to sit across from him.

Nothing about Remy screamed criminal master-mind, though tonight EV had seen the ego-driven, status-seeking, spoiled brat Dalton had described. Without the filter of infatuation clouding it, her vision of him cleared. She saw her past—their past—through new eyes. He'd craved adoration and she'd given it to him, until the new life in her belly had drawn enough of her attention to leave him feeling left of center. He'd turned then—shown her his true self: a petulant child jealous of anything and anyone in his way. Even his unborn baby.

Forward motion slowed while EV processed the

information. Her heart, already closed to him, hardened more. He would not use her again. Ever.

Chapter 9

In the false darkness cast by heavy draperies, EV pulled on her favorite running shoes. There was probably time to get a few miles in before Chloe rose like a specter from the covers EV assumed were currently yanked over her head. Lila's excuse of wanting them both close by hadn't fooled EV one bit. She'd been turned into an unwilling chaperone—a pawn in Lila's game of keep Chloe and Nate apart.

No amount of logic revealed Lila's reasoning for stashing Nate in a room as far away from Chloe as he could be while still remaining inside the castle. EV had thought Lila approved of the match. Worse, it meant sharing a suite with lousy acoustics. Sounds had a way of amplifying from one bedroom to the other. Odd considering the no-expense-spared construction elsewhere in the castle. Given the way sounds echoed, EV had to be quiet in the morning so Princess Lazybones could sleep in.

On her way out the door, EV snagged a bottle of water from the fridge, and her favorite new jacket made of some lightweight, water-resistant material. It kept her dry and warm without making her overly sweaty. Good thing, since the one quick peek she'd risked outside had revealed a lowering gray sky, and the balcony coated in a fine mist.

Following directions in the brochure on her nightstand, EV spent the next hour jogging along the soggy hiking trails located on the west side of the castle. By the time she made her way back to the rooms, the only dry part of her was under that jacket. Too bad it hadn't come with matching pants.

Tossing the wonder garment over a chair, EV grabbed her robe and made a beeline for the bathroom. Chloe was up and gone; probably off somewhere with Lila. That ought to leave enough time for a shower and some breakfast. Just inside the door, she stopped short.

It looked like half a department store makeup aisle had exploded across the small counter. Bottles, brushes, and tubes spread out like casualties after a bombing. Two wet towels lay in a heap on the floor, and in the shower, a complimentary bottle of shampoo leaked its contents down the drain.

Slob.

Ignoring all but the mini-shampoo, EV turned on the shower. At least the water was hot and plentiful, even if the messy room made her eye twitch.

Slamming doors and lilting female voices signaled Chloe's return, letting EV know she wasn't alone. Lila's unmistakable tone penetrated the door as she called out, "Hurry up in there EV, we've got bridesmaid dresses out here."

Whoop-de-doo. EV mentally and physically rolled her eyes. Growing up together, EV remembered Lila's tastes running to pastels, ruffles, and lace—completely opposite from EV's preference for bold colors and simple lines. Still, that was a long time ago. *No hoop skirts. Please, let there be no hoop skirts. Or pink. Or purple. Or lace. On second thought, let me out of this altogether.*

Why did Lila want EV in her wedding to begin with? Yesterday's heart to heart proved how far they'd grown apart over the years. A few phone calls —while nice—didn't a close friendship make, even if the bones were still there. Wasn't there anyone in Lila's swarm of social butterflies who counted a close friend?

Dread kept EV in the bathroom longer than her

normal ten minutes. She straightened up Chloe's mess and generally dawdled until Lila could stand it no longer. Fists pounded on the raised panel, "Get out here or I'm going to pick a dress that makes you look like Barbie's grandmother goes to cotillion."

That did it. EV stepped into the room to see three rolling racks hung to bursting with zippered plastic dress bags.

"Grandmother? I think you mean maiden aunt." EV yanked the door open. "A well-preserved one at that." Her mock glare turned to a genuine grin. "Come on, show us what's in the bags."

Watching Lila open each cocooned bit of froth with such tender excitement made EV's throat tighten with a surge of emotions. If Javier turned out to be the kind of man Chloe was afraid he was, Lila would be devastated. He hadn't scored high on EV's hogwash meter, so she hoped Chloe was wrong. No one could fault him for the way he acted toward Lila—gentle and protective. The only time he had not been forthcoming with information had to do with his family, not with his feelings for Lila.

Shooting a sidelong glance at Chloe, EV pried, "Is Javier's sister going to be in the wedding?"

"Hmm? No, she's not going to be able to get here

until the last minute, so we decided it would be too much hassle."

"And his brothers? Will they be standing up for him?"

"Whoa!" Lila held up a hand. "What's with the third degree?"

"She's just curious about who she's going to be stuck marching with." Chloe stepped in to pull the focus off EV. "But if we're going to be family, I'd at least like to meet some of them. You've spent time with them, right?"

"Of course, I've met his family. His father died when Javi was young, but his mother remarried a lovely man. She's a firecracker. You're going to love her, Chloe. In fact, she reminds me a little bit of you, EV."

"I'm not sure whether to be flattered or creeped out." Wry humor sucked the words dry.

"You should be flattered." Lila turned to unzip the first bag while behind her back, EV and Chloe had one of those conversations that don't require words —only a series of eyebrow raises and subdued gestures. Lila pulled the hanger out of the bag, and that's when EV lost the will to pry.

If there was an ugly Christmas sweater contest

for bridesmaid dresses, this one would win the title hands down. Bright red, with a faux fur band across the strapless top, the black belt and big buckle really did look like something straight from a North Pole closet, but that's where the resemblance ended. Below the belted waistline, the skirt fell in a series of Flamenco dress-type flounces. Mrs. Claus meets Carmen Miranda.

Shock and horror were the words of the day until Lila burst out laughing. "Gotcha."

"That's so not funny," Chloe slapped a hand over her eyes then peered between her fingers. "I think I've been struck blind. Take it away."

But Lila couldn't oblige. She was bent double with laughter, tears welling in the corners of her eyes. Every time she started to regain some semblance of control, another wave hit, until she was gasping for breath. Since she was the one still wearing a robe, EV snatched the dress of the hanger and pulled it over her head. She cha-cha-ed across the floor. By then, Chloe had joined her mother in a bout of tear-filled hooting, and when she reached over the slam the bathroom door shut, EV got a look at herself in the full-length mirror attached to the back.

"I take it this one's a no, then?" EV asked with

feigned seriousness before stripping the dress off and hanging it back in its bag.

She unzipped the next bag far enough to see bubble-gum pink and zipped it right back up again. Lila, finally in control of herself again, shoved EV aside. "Out of the way. I've only seen that one because I had it made as a joke. I'm the bride, I get to look first." She unzipped the same bag EV had just closed, got a look at the color and, just as EV had, zipped it closed with a shudder. "I emailed photos of you both to several boutiques and asked them to send a selection in colors that would complement your skin tones. And yes, EV, that color would look good on either one of you, but I know it's not your thing."

"I'm not the one getting married. If you have your heart set on a hot pink wedding, I'll bite the bullet. Anything for you."

"It's only the second choice, we'll find something we all love." Chloe, of course, liked the color, but wasn't a fan of the sweetheart neckline, so she added her veto to EV's.

• • •

Half an hour later, Chloe, hair standing on end from the static coming off that much plastic, ordered, "Take a break, Mom. I don't know about you, but I'm starving. Call and have some breakfast sent up."

"Two pots of coffee, as per usual?" Lila asked, already knowing the answer. It had probably been a bad idea to perpetuate Chloe's caffeine addiction early on in life. Lila recalled a trip to Brazil around her daughter's 12th birthday where a pre-teen Chloe spent several weeks sipping coffee-laced milk like a native child.

While they waited for room service, Lila seemed unable to help herself, and sorted through several more dress bags. By the time the discreet knock sounded, there was a full rack of rejects, four possibles draped over the back of one chair, and most of two racks left to sort. The waiter pushed a white-draped cart into the room, whisked covers from a series of warming trays, and exited the room.

Chloe wasted no time pouring a cup of coffee and filling a plate. "We got distracted earlier—you were going to tell us about Javier's brother. What does he do?"

Only because she was looking for it, did Chloe see how Lila tensed slightly. "He's in security as well."

"Does he work with Javier?" Lila was holding back, Chloe knew it. EV knew it.

"Not for the last few months."

"I hope they didn't have a falling out."

"There's time to talk about all that later. Let's look at the rest of the options, shall we?" It will be easier to choose flowers when we have dress colors." Lila left her plate of half-eaten food on the table. "We have final choices with the florist right after we finish here."

The sound of a sliding zipper meant the subject was closed. There would be no more prying today.

"Shouldn't the groom be helping choose the flowers?" Okay, there would be a little more prying.

"Javier is doing those system updates today, so he's left that decision in my capable hands."

"Okay then." A new thought struck Chloe. At dinner, Javier had mentioned a theft. Was there some connection between holes in security and his brother?

Lila blew through the second rack like a woman possessed. Only two more dresses made the cut before she started in on the last rack. Watching her mother cast a calculating eye over the contents of each bag, Chloe appreciated her shrewd dress sense. EV could relax, because Lila hadn't been born with the competitive gene. She wanted everyone to look their best at all times. If there was a dress that suited EV's willowy frame while making the most of Chloe's curves, Lila would find it.

Meanwhile, loathe to sit around waiting, Chloe grabbed a bag of possibles and pulled out a dress for EV and one in her size. "How did you know EV's size? You never asked."

"Hmm?" Lila was absorbed in evaluating, "You sent me photos from Halloween."

"She's a savant." Chloe grinned at EV as she handed over a spaghetti-strapped number in dove gray. "If carnivals hired dress size guessers, she'd clean up. I bet it fits perfectly."

"Nothing ever fits perfectly," Lila disagreed. Even on the rare occasion when she wore jeans, she had them tailored.

In this case, she was correct. On EV the dress billowed too loosely over the hip, and Chloe's snugged over the bust. Lila appraised the pair of them.

"That's a no."

The next two garnered a nose wrinkle from Lila, who was halfway through the last rack and had only added another two bags to the dwindling pile of possible choices. She'd better find something soon, or they were going back to square one. Unless there were four more racks somewhere. Chloe wouldn't doubt it.

Something about pulling dresses on and off had affected the static in Chloe's hair; where earlier, it had stood on end, it was now plastered tight to her head. EV's hair had dried every which way to begin with. The dressing and undressing process created further disarray. EV joked, "The only thing missing is raccoon eyes, and we'd look like the morning after a shotgun wedding."

Not liking the comparison, Chloe stomped into the bathroom to rustle around in her things. When she returned, she had a coated hair band and a tube of something. A few deft motions formed her shapeless mass into a charmingly messy chignon, and then, after squeezing a dollop of goo into her hand, she rubbed both hands together and turned on an unsuspecting EV. Moving fast, she ran her hands through EV's hair with a ruffling motion that fluffed it back into attractive messiness.

"There, all better now?"

Lila spared a smile before she went back to perusing options; this was shopping, something she took very seriously.

Three quarters the way through the rack, she finally found a style and color that made her go, "Ooh!"

Lila lifted a spaghetti-strapped silk gown in a shade of blue-gray so muted it was almost silver. Whisper-thin chiffon covered the scalloped bodice in a bust-enhancing criss-cross pattern, and a darker gray, thin velvet sash tied around the ribs.

"I think we have a winner, what do you think?" Lila tossed one dress to Chloe and one to EV. "Try them on."

"A little plain." Chloe raised a skeptical brow.

"Trust me." Lila insisted. "They don't look like much on the hanger, but when you put them on, you'll see. This color will be stunning on Faith as well."

She was right. Even with the wonky hair, Chloe had to admit she looked fantastic, and so did EV.

"I told you, a savant."

Lila circled Chloe, twitched at the fabric at the back of her waist, "A little tuck here, and take the hem up a half inch," she pinched at the top of the wide shoulder strap, "nip this a smidge, and you will be the most beautiful maid of honor to ever walk down the aisle."

She turned to EV, tweaked the material here and there and watched as the small changes subtly enhanced curves that would ordinarily go unnoticed.

"Perfect," Chloe pulled out her phone and snapped a few photos, including a couple selfies. The occasion seemed to call for a duck-lipped shot.

"We're meeting Baylee for lunch, and the florist will come in after that. I need to make a call while you get dressed. Chop chop," Lila called over her shoulder while she rehung the bags of unwanted dresses on their respective racks.

"You don't need me for this part, I'll just..." EV made an attempt to get out of the lunch meeting.

"*We* are meeting Baylee for lunch." Lila emphasized. "And then *we* are going to pick out flowers." Attempt denied. "My dress will arrive by courier tomorrow morning, and I'll want to have my seamstress check the final alterations. She can take measurements for yours, then, too."

"And after that, you can stomp down a few villagers, Bridezilla." EV softened the barb with a smile. "Just think how you'll look in a plaid flannel bridesmaid's dress at my wedding."

"Should fit right in with the hoedown atmosphere—you know, with the pig scramble and all. Just make sure my dress is loose enough not to rip when they fly out of my butt."

"Oh, you are too funny."

"Keep your cop eye on him. I expect a full report when you three get back." Nate recalled Chloe's parting request—if you could call it that—as he, Dalton, and Javier headed to the castle's tailor for tuxedo fittings. Even though Nate wasn't in the wedding, he would inevitably wind up being photographed next to Chloe throughout the event, and Lila wouldn't hear of him attending in anything other than a custom-tailored suit.

By that reasoning, Nate couldn't understand why the same wasn't expected of Dalton. Just one more hoop Lila expected him to navigate. When he spied the decade-old suit his deputy planned to wear, Nate couldn't decide between saying nothing and hoping Lila didn't get a glimpse of it until it was too late, or doing the decent thing and stopping the man from looking like a country cousin. He also made a note to spend time with more male friends when he got back to Ponderosa Pines. This preoccupation with another man's clothing wasn't exactly butch.

"Do you really want to be shown up by Remy Vincent in the wardrobe department, man?"

Dalton blanched. "You're right. I think I'll go with you guys, if you don't mind." Just like that, Nate got what he wanted; maybe it would put Chloe's mind at ease if Dalton could also attest to Javier's character.

Rounding the staircase down to the castle entrance, they spotted Javier leaning casually against the front desk as he chatted with a couple of security staffers. He waved amicably, bid goodbye to the gentlemen behind the counter, and gestured for Nate and Dalton to follow him down a long corridor.

"Come, come. We have quite a walk ahead of us. They manage to put everything a woman would want within arm's reach, while all the amenities designed for men are relegated to dark corners at the far ends of the castle." Javier's accent couldn't be described as thick by any means, but the cadence of his speech combined with somewhat unusual word choices reminded Nate that English was his second language.

"So, your company installed the security system in this place, huh?" Nate asked Javier casually, while shooting a pointed look at Dalton to indicate that this pairing was to double as a reconnaissance mission. Dalton's answering nod proved once again how lucky Nate had gotten when Dalton became a deputy; they required very little communication to be on the same page.

"My technicians handled the installation, yes. My job was to oversee the process, troubleshoot, and sign off on the work."

"That must have been difficult; this place is huge. There must be hundreds of rooms to monitor, not to mention all the places guests aren't allowed access. Are all the staff areas monitored as well? What kind of crew did it take to complete a job this big?" Dalton's questions didn't seem to phase Javier; the three had crossed the line into Man Territory, where it was perfectly acceptable to discuss the technical aspects of their work.

Javier grinned, and launched into detail without hesitation. "There are a few remote areas that aren't monitored with video; those are secured with other methods. And of course, there are no cameras in the guest rooms, or in any of the restrooms or changing areas; that would be a breach of privacy. My crew includes five upper-level security experts, who report directly to me. Each of them supervised a team of six technicians along with the requisite craftsmen needed to maintain the ambiance. Even still, the job took nearly four months. I've seen every nook and cranny of this place. More than once."

Both Nate and Dalton were intrigued at this point; they would have continued digging for information regardless of whether they had been asked to do so. Spurred on by their eager expressions of avid interest, Javier continued rambling on.

"The cameras are actually a small part of the system, though there are over two hundred positioned throughout the public areas of the castle, and thanks to some local artisans, they are virtually undetectable unless you know to look for them." Javier stopped to point out what looked like a pinhole in the cornice above them.

"They're the eyes, but without the mainframe—or brain, as I like to describe it—they're useless. All of that information is recorded, backed up, and compiled in the event that it needs to be reviewed. The castle's permanent security team monitors certain areas continuously—mostly high-traffic parts of the castle—but the rest is only accessed when the cameras detect movement. We also installed a new key card system, not only for guest rooms, but also for staff. Everyone is assigned a photo ID badge; they each hold a chip that grants access to certain areas, depending on that person's clearance level."

"Undetectable? Then I assume you must get some very interesting footage. People often do the strange when they think no one is looking," Nate mused.

A quick grin flashed across Javier's face. "On that, we are agreed. You must see plenty of that type of thing in your own line of work."

"I did when I worked in Portland. Ponderosa Pines has its own brand of weird, but it's very subdued."

"Most of the time," Dalton reminded him, "we had some outside strange come to town recently." He and Nate between them went on to describe the invasion of the Sasquatch hunters, their inevitable rout, and Chloe's part in driving them away.

"Now that would have been worth seeing," Javier allowed amiably.

Feeling more comfortable now that they had shared some bonding experience, Nate asked, "How did you happen to get into the security business?"

Apparently, Javier's candidness was exclusive to discussing only the technical side of things, he side-stepped the personal aspect of the conversation adeptly. "That's a long story, for another time. We have arrived." Whatever nefarious intent Chloe thought she sensed in the man, Nate wasn't seeing anything other than a desire for personal privacy.

In contrast to Lila's time-intensive focus on choosing the correct wedding finery, Nate and Dalton made their decisions rapidly with a minimum of fuss. An hour and a half saw all three men enjoying a Guinness in the pub. Nothing—but nothing—would induce any one of them to go looking for the women until absolutely certain the dress choosing was over.

Chapter 10

"Come with me, I know a private place where we won't be found." Chloe tugged at Nate's hand, leading him around a corner and through a door marked for staff use only. She had an hour—two tops—away from Lila and wedding planning; she intended to make the most of that time.

"Lead the way!"

Several more twists and turns deposited the pair in a deserted hallway. Sconces adorned the rough stone walls every few feet, ancient dried wax dripping from the candle holders. Rejected portraits of past ruling family members quietly decomposed on the walls; these particular pieces had been commissioned by less talented artists. Something about them just seemed off—a too-long nose here, an unsightly mole overemphasized there—or perhaps the renderings had been too close to reality, and therefore relegated to dark corners out of self-consciousness.

"This is the section of the castle the staff uses for storage. There's a balcony up ahead; should be deserted."

Nate performed a quick search and officially cleared the area, then pulled Chloe behind a curtain and began nuzzling her neck. A low moan escaped his lips as her fingers brushed lightly between the waist of his slacks and the taut line of his stomach muscles. Before the tryst could turn into anything serious, they heard a voice ringing out from somewhere above.

Chloe released herself from Nate's grip and shuffled quietly toward the balcony's edge. He grasped her by the wrist and pulled her back into the shadows, finger to his lips to let her know that silence was necessary. She returned his gesture with a hand wave meant to convey the sentiment, *duh.*

"That's Javier. He must be directly above us." Nate whispered. His cop instincts took over, letting him know there was a reason to listen to the conversation that must have been important enough to carry Javier to this remote area of the castle. They both stood still as statues, muscles tensed, straining to make out every word of the conversation.

"... disabled, you'll have five minutes. That should be enough time. Are you positive you want to go ahead with this? It could be dangerous. No. I said I would help, and I won't back out now. Yes, the safe, too. Yes. I'll be ready. Win or lose, this is it—our last chance. I want this to be my last job. I fully intend to spend the rest of my life next to a sandy beach some-where...yeah, I know I hit the jackpot. Okay, be ready, and wait for my signal."

Chloe didn't breathe until Javier had retreated into the upstairs room, and didn't speak until they had followed the path back to the main part of the castle. Her cheeks flamed red as Nate stabbed the up arrow next to a small bank of elevators; he could tell she was about to launch into a patented Chloe-rant.

"Wait until I get my hands on that slimy bast—" Nate's lips softly interrupted her tirade, but she was angry enough to break the kiss before it turned into a distraction.

"Let's find Dalton and EV, and then you can start plotting his demise. For now, we need to keep this to ourselves. We don't know what's actually going on; let's not jump to conclusions or be overheard by anyone." He chastised gently, looking pointedly at the few guests milling about the hallway.

Chloe held her tongue until all four of them had assembled in Nate's room, where Lila's prying eyes and curious ears wouldn't interrupt the conversation. EV and Dalton, assuming the urgent matter that had dragged them from a few moments of hard-earned serenity had to do with Remy, sat side by side. His face mirrored her expression of resignation. As soon as Chloe's tirade began, they both relaxed for a moment before reacting to this newest twist.

"That son of a bitch, Javier, is up to no good! Nate and I were, um, exploring some of the more remote parts of the castle..." her eyes flicked to Nate, who bore a sheepish expression of his own, and quickly continued, "when we overheard a conversation between him and someone on the other end of the phone. He's planning some kind of break in—he's going to abuse his position in security to steal something from someone, and then he's going to screw over my mother and take all her money. This isn't the first time he's ripped someone off, either; he said this was his last job, and that he was planning on retiring on some beach with all of his cash! We have to take him down; he won't get away with this!" Chloe began pacing back and forth, muttering under her breath.

"Are you sure that's what's going on?" Dalton, always able to see both sides of a story, wondered out loud, directing the question toward Nate.

"I hate to admit it, but it seemed pretty cut and dried to me."

"Great, now we have two situations to deal with. And Lila seemed so happy. This is going to crush her." EV lamented.

"I'm not sure there's anything I can do about this; we have no jurisdiction here, and it's not like I can go to the head of security and ask for help." Nate swiped a hand through his hair for about the tenth time; he was beginning to look like a troll doll from the '90's. "Dalton and I'll keep an eye on him, but he's got more resources than we do. Man, I really thought he was a good guy. The only other course of action we can take is to tell Lila."

"EV and I will take that particular bullet. C'mon, let's see if we can find her."

Miles of hallways, dozens of rooms, and fifty acres of grounds made tracking down any single guest into a chore. Not to mention, Lila had a long list of errands and a jam-packed wedding planning schedule, so there was no telling where she had run off to.

"Her cell goes straight to voicemail, as usual. I just love how when she wants to get a hold of *me*, I'm expected to answer on the first ring, but she doesn't even have the presence of mind to keep her phone on her. And, at a time like this, with a million things to do, and calls to make. Damn my mother!" Chloe's earlier irritation was now hitting record levels; the thunder clouds hovering above her head were swirling; a lightening clap threatening to sound at any moment. EV didn't particularly want to be around when it did, having witnessed several of Chloe's meltdowns already. Her bark was always worse than her bite; once Chloe unloaded, she turned back into a cuddly puppy. Nothing festered too long, but the anticipation of when she would finally snap was enough to drive EV mad.

"Let's go back to our suite and see if she's there. Maybe she left her tablet in her room; we can check her agenda and track her down."

But there was no need; as they passed by the atrium dining room, Chloe stopped dead in her tracks. Lila was sitting at a table by the window—the best one in the house—wedding planning materials spread all around her. Most guests would have been ushered into a less public room for this type of task, but then, most guests weren't Lila LaRue. An impeccably-pressed waiter stood nearby, poised to jump at the smallest command.

Noting Lila's dreamy expression as she scanned over a list of table setting options, EV's stomach dropped at the thought of disappointing her old friend. Though it had to be done, she would have preferred not to be the bearer of bad news.

"Hey Mom, can we sit?" Chloe shifted her weight awkwardly from one foot to another, almost hoping to be turned away and avoid the situation altogether.

"Of course, dear. Would you like something to eat? Or a drink, perhaps? Claude here will get you anything you'd like." Lila cleared a space at the table for each of them, setting another pile of paperwork and samples onto the remaining empty chair beside her.

Chloe settled onto the proffered seat and held up a hand, discouraging the eager waiter. "No, thank you. We need to talk to you. It's about Javier." She turned to the waiter, "Could you give us a moment?"

"What about him, darling, don't you like him?" Lila's starry eyes every time she talked about Javier cut Chloe like a knife. This was going to be difficult. She looked to EV for support, received a gentle nod of encouragement, and launched into her story. Instead of outrage, Lila appeared bewildered by the accusation that Javier was planning to breach security.

"You're jumping to conclusions. He's been on the phone practically every spare minute today discussing those inaccurate break-in reports. This kind of thing happens all the time at hotels; it's his job to investigate, and I'm sure what you overheard had to do with that."

Chloe considered the question, but couldn't help remembering the urgency in Javier's tone, the mention of danger, and the comment about disabling a safe. That didn't seem to be on the up-and-up to her. When she didn't answer, Lila continued.

"Chloe, do you honestly think that I can't take care of myself, after all this time? And do you really think I would get into a marriage—at my age, and with my assets—without truly knowing the man? Or without a prenup? Javier has plenty of money of his own, and we have plans to buy a beach house. That must have been what he was talking about. Now, stop worrying about me, and give him a chance. I think you'll really like him once you get to know him.

Can't you just be happy that I'm happy? I thought you would have wanted more for me, and I'm disappointed that you're not being supportive. You're so dramatic, Chloe, and it's unbecoming. Now, if you'll excuse me, I need to finalize these table setting choices. I'll see you at dinner tonight."

Lila went back to flipping through the hand bound portfolio, pointedly keeping her gaze away from Chloe and EV's. The fact that her reaction sounded an awful lot like one of Chloe's own tirades did not escape EV, but she knew better than to comment. Still, she wasn't known for keeping her mouth shut, and couldn't help but interject.

"Lila, we're only trying to look out for you. We aren't here to question your judgment; I know from experience that it's easy to believe in someone and then find out their intentions aren't in your best interests."

"Mother, please. I love you, and I don't want anything bad to happen to you." Chloe implored.

"I have it covered." Was Lila's response. "Now please, butt out." And with that, she refused to say another word, forcing Chloe to retreat, pulling EV alongside.

"I don't know what we were thinking,

approaching her that way. She's as stubborn as a mule; it's clear where you picked up that charming trait." A gentle hand on Chloe's shoulder took the sting out of the accusation, though she knew EV was right. There was only one way to get through to Lila now—expose Javier. Now they just needed a plan.

Chapter 11

"I've seen how you look at him; how your eyes search him out!" Dalton railed at EV.

A wave of her hand dismissed his concerns, "You're letting your imagination get the better of you."

Fists clenched, Dalton kicked the leg of the lounge chair nearest him—a little harder than he'd meant to. It slid about a foot across the flagstones, making a horrendous screeching noise as it did.

"How mature." EV commented, the wry twist of her lips that matched his chagrined grimace at odds with the glint in her eye.

"Mature? You're questioning my maturity level when you're practically panting after your high school sweetheart! Tell me, EV, has it been a strain on your arms to carry that torch all this time?" He let his voice rise up a decibel or two.

"I guess you'll have to tell me. Is that why your

wife left you? Because she couldn't stand watching you pant after me all those years?" Her shrill words carried on the wind.

"Leave Marlene out of this. She had her own reasons for leaving, and they didn't have anything to do with you. In fact, lots of things happen in Ponderosa Pines that have nothing to do with you! Too bad you can't seem to stay out of anything that goes on, though." He reached forward to poke her in the chest. She leaned into it, forcing him to pull back a little at the last second. He'd left her the perfect opening.

"Tell that to the Elders who can't seem to do squat without running it by me first! I've been here four days, and they've called seven times to ask inane questions." She injected, her voice rife with loathing.

"You've got a lot of nerve complaining about having to make decisions when it's your control issues that make you think you're in charge of every-thing. *I'm* law enforcement. It was *my* job to find Evan Plunkett's killer, and you couldn't even let me have that much room on my chain. You had to go and do it for me." EV saw a hint of actual resentment still lingering in him about that one, although she still maintained the timing had been against her.

"Evan Plunkett. Hah!! You were floundering around with no clue, so I had to step in and handle things. Like I always do." It was her turn to poke him in the chest. "You should be thanking me, not throwing it in my face!"

Dalton pulled it back from taking the argument to a more real place. Finding her in her own home facing the wrong end of a gun was an image he would probably never get out of his head.

"Maybe if you let me take my balls out of your purse once in a while, I'd get something done."

The visual on that one was nearly EV's undoing, but she held it together even though her eyes were alight with amusement.

"Fine, you want 'em? I'm through with you and your balls!" EV swung on her heel and stalked away, leaving Dalton standing there for a moment before he, too, stomped off in the other direction.

From where he stood, conveniently hidden behind one of the battlements above the terrace, Remy listened with a smarmy, self-satisfied smirk, and no clue that the entire scene had been staged for his benefit.

EV would be headed back to her room to change into running gear. He'd bet it was still her preferred method of blowing off steam. If he hurried, he could probably intercept her. The smirk turned to a leer. There were other ways an angry woman could channel her emotions. If he was lucky, he might just *get lucky* with her. "Jerk alert. Behind you," Chloe leaned against one of the columns in the foyer; she hissed the warning to EV when she passed by. In answer, EV waggled her eyebrows and put a little extra sway into her step that didn't match the black look on her face. Making the quick decision to keep to public spaces, she stepped into the homey little pub. More than one head turned to watch her pass.

Plunking down on a tufted bar stool, EV rested her elbows on mahogany with an inch-thick finish polished to a gleam. "Scotch rocks," she barked at the bartender. Poor man, he didn't deserve to be dragged into this.

She felt, rather than saw Remy ooze onto the next stool over—schooled the lip that wanted to curl when his thigh brushed against hers. As it was, he took the shiver running through her as an indication of interest, rather than the revulsion it actually signified.

Asshat follies, act two.

"Here we are again. Face it, EV. Fate keeps drawing you to me."

What? Like flies to a fresh pile? "Go away, Remy. I'm in no mood to deal with you right now."

"You don't want me to leave. We both know that."

I'd better get an Oscar for this.

EV let her eyes fill with tears and said, "I'd really like to be alone." In the past, playing the hero had been his favorite role. Assuming some things never change, she tapped into his fantasy.

"Man trouble? You need someone to cheer you up. I'm just the guy. Do you still like to dance?" He pulled her out on the floor. This early in the evening, it was practically empty. Only one other couple occupied the space. EV let a smile hover as she watched a dapper gentleman in his mid-seventies with nimble feet twirl his wife out and back, then bend her into a dip that ended in a kiss.

"Loosen up." Remy admonished, when EV remained stiff in his arms.

"I'd rather just go back to my room." For once, her thoughts and her words matched.

"We'd have more privacy if we went to mine."

Not if you were the last man on earth.

"Why are you here? After all this time, what's behind this compulsion you seem to have for mending fences? Lila says you two have managed to successfully avoid each other for years, despite running in similar circles. So, why now?"

"I came for you, EV. When I heard Lila was getting married, I knew you'd come. I had to see you."

"Why? We don't even know each other any more."

"I've never forgotten you. Us. You can't tell me you don't remember how good we were together."

I think I threw up in my mouth a little.

"I remember." EV let her body loosen and become more pliant. She dropped her head onto his shoulder. He pulled her more tightly against his body; dipped his head to bring his lips closer to hers.

Nope, nope, nope. There's a limit.

EV pulled back, pushing him away. "I can't be with you right now, I need to go." She let him think she was torn by her own desire for him. With his ego running rampant, he reached that conclusion on the tiniest of leaps.

In the rush of getting away from Remy while she still had enough control to keep from breaking cover and telling him exactly what a jackass he really was, she passed right by Dalton, who glowered in the shadows. He, however, had no problem giving Remy a piece of his mind.

With EV clear of the room, Remy returned to the bar, a smirk on his face. No way he could lose now. This should have been his plan all along. What better way to take down the community he hated than by turning their own figurehead against them. All he had to do was get her into bed; get her addicted to him again. She'd do anything to please him, just like before. He wondered if she was still a tiger in the sack —maybe he would take his time with it. Inject the poison slowly, then watch her burn Ponderosa Pines to the ground. Figuratively, of course.

Too busy gloating, he paid no attention to the man who slid onto the barstool recently vacated by his prey. When Dalton's voice sounded in his ear, Remy twitched in surprise.

"If you hurt her, I'll kill you." There was no threat in the words, only a promise.

"Look at you, Ernie Burnie," Remy sneered. Dalton let the insult pass. He wasn't interested in reverting to childish name calling. "She'll choose me. Just like she did the first time. I won then; I'll do it again."

"If you hurt her, I'll take you apart in little pieces, and hide them where no one will ever think to look." Dalton repeated.

"You don't scare me, Burnsoll. One word from me, and you'll go sniveling off in a corner like you always did." Remy's dismissal pushed Dalton's buttons.

"Time passes. Things change. I'm all grown up now, Remy. Too bad I can't say the same for you. EV's mine now. You had your chance with her, and you blew it."

"Maybe you should tell her that, so she'll stop sniffing around. I don't think you can hold her."

The image of Remy's head rocking back as Dalton pumped fists into his face rose up in Dalton like a siren's song. Several deep breaths passed before he felt fully controlled enough to get up and walk away. His parting shot, "Remember what I said."

If he'd thought the confrontation would release the angry pressure he felt whenever that scumbag was in the room, Dalton had been wrong. The argument had made it ten times worse.

Chapter 12

The jingling of her phone for about the fifth time in as many hours elicited an internal groan from Chloe. She was sure it was Talia again, with another photo update on how Sugar and Spice were doing while she was away. *For crying out loud, I love them, but they're cats.* Sure enough, her inbox showed another new message featuring a picture of Sugar and Spice curled up together on a fluffy sage green ottoman Chloe recognized as part of Talia's living room furniture.

Not bothering with even a perfunctory response, Chloe instead opened the group message including Veronica and Mindy. Four unanswered texts all wanted the same info; those two had one-track minds—well, maybe two-track. First, the intimate details of what they imagined was a romantic getaway for her and Nate; second, to ensure that Chloe wasn't screwing up the relationship in their absence. Chloe suspected a significant part of the second was related to concern that she'd be leaving them without another full couple for future game nights if the relationship went south.

I'm in bridal hell, and my mother is wielding the pitchfork. Not a lot of time for extracurriculars, but we're making the best of it. Girls' night when I get back; the entire story is going to require many mojitos and about three pounds of fudge. Miss you!

She knew they'd be clamoring for more, and as she silenced her phone Chloe's mind began to wander back to Ponderosa Pines. This trip, supposed to be fun and relaxing, had turned into anything but. Right now, she would rather be curled up in her own bed next to Nate—all thoughts of Remy, Javier, and high crime expunged from her memory.

To top it all off, her editor, Wesley, had insisted she write at least one current edition of 'Babble & Spin', in case anyone noticed a correlation between the timing of her absence and the lack of an original column. She and Wesley had concocted a plan—initially Chloe's idea—of releasing several "throw-back" editions of the paper during the rest of her vacation. Each would feature news from the past, in what Wesley had coined a *Retro-Spective*. The chosen articles would reflect a theme; any new pieces high-lighting the changes that had taken place between the past and the present.

It was a good plan—one people would enjoy—but one that required her to get creative. Luckily, EV's cell was burning up with a slew of text messages detailing all of the goings-on back home, and though the residents of Ponderosa Pines fancied themselves above most of the high-tech nonsense, they were all just as hooked on social media as the rest of the country.

Although Chloe typically followed up on leads gleaned from sites like Facebook and Instagram in person, she figured one column of recycled information wouldn't hurt anyone. Everyone else was occupied with their own tasks at the moment, and since Nate still didn't know about her secret job title, it was as good a time as any to get it out of the way—one less thing she'd have to worry about.

After scouring the web for useful information, Chloe combined her findings with the texts EV had deemed useful to pen a short but informative column.

Hey Piniacs, are you ready to dish? Looks like we're rudderless without our fearless leader. Miss Grapevine herself is off living it up in style at an Irish castle. Hope she and her side-kick are having a great time. We're all on the edge of our seats wondering about Lila LaRue's new fiancé. Hope they're taking lots of pics for us homebodies!

Meanwhile, back on the ranch, Lottalia are making folks uncomfortable everywhere they go—can't sisters just get along? It's old news that Lofty Lottie has always lorded over little 'sis; guess she's having trouble now that Teeny Tallie's grown a monster-sized pair. Maybe what's private should remain behind closed doors, huh ladies?

Chloe pushed aside the modicum of guilt she felt at calling out two people she actually considered friends, especially one who was doing her a big favor at that very moment. Still, their antics were getting out of control, and she was just carrying on the decades-old tradition of unrelenting snark Wesley expected of her. Besides, maybe a little public humiliation would encourage Lottie to back off her newly-widowed sister.

By the time the task was complete, Chloe felt a weight lift from her shoulders; partially because she could now focus on what was in front of her, but mostly because she had made the decision to come clean with Nate, and let him know that she was the author of 'Babble & Spin'. She only hoped he wasn't too mad at her for keeping the secret in the first place.

Just about to power down her laptop, an errant thought struck Chloe. She checked her watch; Lila and Javier were occupied with couples-only wedding tasks, so she had at least an extra half hour to herself, and decided to put it to good use.

What's your end game, Hannah Frank?

She opened several browser tabs and searched a few keywords related to Hannah Frank, HF Designs, and the scandal that had ejected her from Hollywood's inner circle.

If there was one area in which the woman excelled, it was public relations; the entire first two pages of every phrase Chloe searched turned up links to Hannah's wedding planning website, her Twitter and Facebook accounts, and several newer reports touting her many achievements. Since most people didn't bother to click any further, prospective clients were likely to miss the scathing articles and reviews that followed. Chloe wasn't most people; gossip was her bread and butter, so she scoured Hannah's Facebook page and found even more evidence of a cover-up.

Her company, HF Designs, had undergone an overhaul; it used to be called Hannah Frank, Inc. Still based out of Los Angeles, the new site merely hinted at celebrity clients, focusing mainly on showcasing Hannah's exceptional event planning skills. She was obviously focused on rebuilding; Lila LaRue didn't qualify as a celebrity in most circles, but her vast resources would enable Hannah to display recent work on a Hollywood-worthy wedding. If only she could edge her way into the planning process.

The question was, why was she ousted in the first place? Sure, celebrities could be fickle, but a scandal of the caliber Lila described had to be based on more than just a minor infraction. With a little more time for research, Chloe was sure she could turn up some-thing juicy—time being the one thing she lacked right now. Switching tactics, Chloe tapped out a hurried email request to Wesley, her editor back in

Ponderosa Pines, whose research skills rivaled her own. In a series of short sentences, she told him what she needed, gave him the links to the sites she'd already searched and asked him to do the legwork.

Lila had a lot going on at the moment; this was something Chloe could do on her own. Well, with a little help from her friends, anyway.

"How much do you love me?" Chloe asked with unusual sweetness.

EV grimaced and quirked her right eyebrow. "Enough. What do you want?" She sipped a cup of Irish tea, her hair blowing in the cool breeze wafting against the suite's west-facing balcony as a dazzling sun set over the horizon. In the distance, a brilliant blue lake kissed the shining rays, coloring the sky in pink and purple stripes. EV tore her eyes away from the scene reluctantly, and shot an inquiring look at her friend. Chloe was distracted, barely noticing the picturesque view that lay before her.

"A small favor. Could you get Lila away from the suite for a few hours around dinner time—distract her so I can have some alone time with Nate."

"Seriously? You guys are like bunny rabbits." She rolled her eyes, but behind her rueful facade she was genuinely happy. EV had never seen Chloe this ecstatic about a man; it was a good look for her. But, for crying out loud, how much alone time did those two need?

Chloe swatted her arm playfully. "Get your mind out of the gutter. I need to talk to him is all. It's time I told him my secret. He should at least know what I do for a living—if you can call it that—if we're going to pursue a real relationship. And I trust him. I just hope he understands why I didn't say anything before." Whether she was required to or not, lying was lying, and she knew Nate valued honesty above all other virtues.

"I'm guessing he'll get it. I'd be more concerned that he's pissed about you referring to him as *Inspector Hottie* all the time."

"Yeah, on second thought, maybe I'll just keep my lips zipped." Chloe had heard Nate complain about the term of endearment several times, and was mildly ashamed at the fact that she had continued to do so mostly just to irritate him. She figured he deserved it, after letting her believe he was dating a woman who turned out to be a co-worker and friend. Jealousy did not become her, and Chloe's angry response had set them back even further before Dalton had clued her in on the truth.

"Well, maybe butter him up a little bit first, then. I'll take care of your mother." After Lila's reaction to the warning about her *fiancé*, EV wasn't keen on the idea of spending the evening with the two of them alone. "You'll owe me."

"Yeah, yeah. Add it to my bill." Chloe waved a dismissive hand.

Chapter 13

Was it really hacking into the system if he was the one who designed it? Gray area, but when family is on the line, you do whatever it takes. Javier's fingers flew over his laptop keyboard while he tamped down the twinges his conscience kept throwing at him. Baylee's last text before silencing her phone said she was in place, so he keyed in the sequence to unlock Remy Vincent's room remotely, and started the countdown on his watch.

They'd given themselves a five-minute window. Javier pictured Baylee slipping through the door, flipping on the light, rifling through Vincent's things to find something—anything—that would prove he was the identity thief responsible for framing Tomas and destroying his life.

Four and a half minutes left.

He marked the time, starting the countdown to the next stage of the plan. Baylee had one minute to orient herself, then be ready for the room safe to unlock in four, three, two—Javier tapped the enter key. Now she would be pulling open the door, rifling through the contents, and clicking photos of anything she found. He waited the allotted two minutes before reengaging the lock. Two minutes more for her to check the rest of the room and get out.

Time crawled past while he waited, finger poised to execute the command that would lock the door behind her—all the while knowing that for Baylee, the same five minutes must be whizzing past.

When the digital timer clicked to zero, Javier pushed the enter key with an unsteady finger. Baylee had agreed to a second foray if this one turned up nothing, but Javier wasn't sure he could do it again. If this much adrenaline was surging through his veins, how much more would be turning Baylee into a jittery mess?

Javier spent another five minutes erasing all evidence that Vincent's lock had been activated from the system. Baylee should have checked back in by now. Cold dread settled into his belly when he pinged her cell and got no response.

Now what? Should he stay here and prepare to clear the history if she had needed to trigger the lock again, or should he go look for her?

It was already too late, but Javier had no way of knowing that.

Baylee checked the hallway in both directions, watched the red light on the video camera flicker and go out. To her right, the soft click of the door lock deactivating sounded louder to her ears than it should have. With a glance over her shoulder to make sure the coast was still clear, she slid inside. All the rooms in this section were laid out the same, only the fabric and paint choices differentiated one from another.

Bathroom to the right, closet to the left. Beyond that, a small seating area took up the left side of the room, with a compact executive workspace in the far corner. A king-sized bed flanked by a pair of night-stands rested along the right hand wall. The night-stand closest to the door contained a small safe. That was the most likely place to find what she was after, but to be thorough, she quickly checked the closet and desk area for a laptop or briefcase that might hold additional evidence.

Finding neither, she turned to the safe, counted down the seconds until the lock clicked open.

Javier had been right, this Remy Vincent character really had been behind everything that had happened to turn her husband's life—and hers, by extension—into a smoking ruin. She spread the documents on the floor, snapped several photos of them, then packed it all back into the safe, being careful to conceal any evidence of the search.

With thirty seconds to go, Baylee flipped the door that concealed the safe closed, and double-checked that nothing appeared out of place. Satisfied, she exited the room.

Adrenaline rushed through her—narrowing her focus to a small point while everything else blurred, quickening the breath in her body—that was the only excuse she had for not noticing Remy standing there. When he called out, "Hey, what are you doing?" She let the juice flow through her and took off at a sprint.

Remy gave chase; legs longer than hers eating up the distance. Baylee knew she was sunk. Fumbling while she ran, the pulled the SIM card from the camera; her only thought now was to hide the evidence somewhere she could retrieve it later. He was older, out of shape, so she used the last burst of adrenaline to put on some speed and turned the corner with extra space between them. If she could get back to the more populated area of the castle, maybe someone would help her.

She made it out of the south wing, feet flying down the short staircase that would get her back onto the level of her own room. Turning into the west wing of the castle, she wondered *where was everyone?* Behind her, his feet pounded toward the stairs; getting louder as he began to close the gap.

Scanning the area with frantic eyes, she saw only one possible place to hide the SIM card. She lost a few precious seconds, but when it was done, she knew he would never find it.

The hallway ended in a T. Baylee searched her mind for which direction to take, and that was her fatal mistake. She dodged right, and when the hallway turned left again, found herself racing toward a dead end. There was no way she was going to escape now. She turned to face her fate.

Behind her, Remy panted out the evidence of his lack of physical fitness. Baylee estimated that if she could get past him, she could make it back to the intersection of the T and double her lead.

"What were you doing in my room?" Sweat beaded on his brow from the same exertion that reddened his face and shortened his breath.

Baylee gauged the distance with her eyes, without realizing she had telegraphed her plan. Rising onto the balls of her feet, she launched into a sprint which ended abruptly when he sidestepped to clothesline her. Carpeted, though they were, the heavy stone floors underneath were unyielding, so when Baylee landed, the blow to her head stunned her into complacency. She felt him lift her with more strength than she would have given him credit for, and the world tilted, then grayed to black.

The next clear thought Baylee had was that someone must be driving nails into her skull. She wished they would stop. Temple throbbing, she tried to lift her hand, to press fingers against the pulsing pain, but something was weighing it down. Her eyes fluttered partially open, then closed tightly again. She cataloged the places where she ached. Her head, her neck, her shoulders. Full awareness returned slowly, bringing with it the memory of a desperate flight ending in pain and darkness.

Remy.

Her eyes snapped open. With her photographer's insight into human emotion, she knew the look on his face had been fear rather than anger. That made him more dangerous, because a fearful man will usually go to greater lengths than an angry one. Fully alert now, Baylee absorbed her surroundings. Dust, piles of building materials, a dimly lit light fixture, and the abject lack of noise suggested she was in one of the older, not yet renovated parts of the castle.

And she was tied up.

Panic set in, and though each movement tightened her bonds, Baylee couldn't stop struggling against them. She opened her mouth to scream for help when from behind her, Remy's voice made her jump. She'd thought herself alone.

"Don't scream, no one will hear you anyway, and I'm not going to hurt you if you cooperate." Remy's smarmy face was equally unpleasant as his whiny voice; even if Baylee had no preconceived notion of his repulsiveness, she would have steered clear of the man. How someone so obviously incompetent had managed to wreak so much havoc was beyond her, and she briefly wondered if some kind of deal with the devil had been made.

She heard footsteps and looked from where he'd placed her—on the floor, tied to a support beam. Remy carried her camera in his hands. "Who are you and why were you spying on me?"

Should she tell him, and hope he would let her go? Or should she trust Javier to handle the situation and find her? Remy's next words didn't help with the decision.

"Where's the memory card? Give it to me, or tell me where it is, and I'll let you go."

EV knocked on Lila's door while her busy mind searched for some believable pretense for keeping Lila out of Chloe's way for and hour or so. A pointed text from Chloe settled the matter:

Um, forgot about Dalton. Tell me where you'll be so I can send him to you.

I'm next door now, not sure yet—was all the answer she had time for before the door flew open.

"Can I come in? If you have time, I was hoping we could go to dinner in the café. Dalton, too." She looked past Lila to see if Javier was in the room. "I'd love a chance to just visit with you. Talk about old times."

"Did Chloe send you here to give Javi the third degree?" Lila was only half right.

"Can't I just want to catch up and spend some time with my oldest friend without you picking apart my motives?" Lila cocked her head, searched EV for signs of prevarication and finding none, relented.

"Fine." A slight chill still wafted through her voice. "Javi should be back by now." Lila swung the door the rest of the way open, glanced down the hallway to see him turn the corner at the end of the hall. When he was near enough to hear, she said, "Javi, sweetie, we're going to dinner with Dalton and EV who, if they know what's good for them, will not reveal any of my youthful indiscretions."

A glance back in the direction from which he'd come and the slowness of his steps spoke of Javier's reluctance to be pulled away from whatever it was he'd been doing.

"Though I'd like to hear some of those; regrettably, I have an errand." Coming up behind EV, Javier's even teeth gleamed impossibly white in contrast to his olive-hued skin. He laid a hand on

Lila's shoulder, giving it a gentle squeeze. The look on his face did not immediately mirror Lila's shining eyes and foolish grin. Instead, stress wrote lines around his eyes, until she squeezed his hand, and a more genuine smile appeared. That he was hiding something, EV had no doubt, but it wasn't his true feelings for Lila.

"Can't it wait, Dear? I've hardly seen you all day." Lila in full-on persuasive mode was impossible to resist. Torn between the desire to keep looking for Baylee, and the need for everything to seem like business as usual, Javier relented. Maybe she'd had to duck in somewhere to avoid detection, and was just waiting to get clear before texting him.

"I can delay for a short time," he allowed, as he followed EV and Lila inside and closed the door behind him. The three of them had just enough time to take a seat before Dalton's discreet knock halted the conversation and Lila yanked the door open and pulled him in for a welcoming hug.

"Just remember," Lila wagged a finger at EV, "Whatever embarrassing stories I have, you were right there beside me."

"True, but you were always the one with the best ideas, I was just the gullible follower." EV pasted an exaggerated look of innocence on her face, but Lila only hooted.

Dalton snorted. "I was the bystander; you two were forces of nature."

"What about that time you stole a bottle of Zellner's famous strawberry wine and we…" Javier leaned in a little closer to hear the revelation. "Never mind."

The four took the stairs down toward the café on the second level of the atrium.

A charming wrought iron, glass-topped table sat in a patch of watery light. To their left, the view out the large expanse of glass showed another misty day, the sky not just threatening rain, but promising it. From what EV could tell, that was most days this time of year.

Out of the corner of her eye, Lila caught sight of a familiar head of curly blond hair. She let out a low, involuntary hiss and locked eyes with Hannah Frank. Camera phone poised, the quick flash netted her a photo of nothing but Lila's most hateful scowl. Another pointed look sent Hannah scurrying toward the café exit, her mouth set in a grim, frustrated line. Lila returned her attention to the table; none of her companions had witnessed the exchange, so she shoved irritation aside and focused on the conversation at hand.

Talk turned to Ponderosa Pines, while EV and Dalton entertained with the story of how Sasquatch hunters had come to visit their small town. Lila nearly busted a gut laughing as EV described Chloe rising like a wild Yeti ghost and giving them the sharp side of her tongue. Javier's laughter felt a little forced—EV would have sworn he hadn't heard half the story; too busy looking his phone as though willing it to make some kind of signal.

"If you'll excuse me, I need to make a call." Javier moved away from the table. There was no answer from Baylee, so he typed a quick text message.

All clear?

Lila watched him go with barely-masked concern. "What about your parents, are they well? They must be in their early seventies by now. It's been such a long time since I've seen them." She directed at EV.

"They're doing fine. Father finally gave in and turned the foundation over to cousin George four years ago, though he still keeps his hand in when he can."

Javier bumped into the table on his return. Lila

glanced up with concern, but he composed his features into an expression of interest at the current conversation and ignored her silent question.

"Mother has slowed down, probably because he is a constant distraction, but she continues to produce one or two new pieces every year." EV spoke to Lila, but remained acutely aware of Javier's expression.

Lila turned to Javier, "It's a family secret, but EV's mother goes by her maiden name in the art world: Anna Zemaya."

"She would be the genius behind the tapestry in your bedroom, correct?"

Lila nodded. "Her use of color is exceptional."

"Which piece?" EV asked.

"Willow Sky." Lila waved her fork. "I picked it up in a gallery in..."

"San Francisco." EV finished for her. "I'll tell you one of my biggest secrets—I've been working as my mother's agent for the last fifteen years."

Surprise lifted Lila's brows. "I had no idea. That must have meant a fair amount of travel for you."

"Less these past few years, but yes; I haven't spent my life chained to a pine tree." A hint of bitterness crept into her voice. Lila's lips tightened as she asked Dalton about his family.

He patted EV on the knee before answering with a grin, "Older but no wiser. My dad went bungee jumping last year." He gave a little shiver thinking about it. Of all the things passed down from his father—long earlobes, funny looking middle toe, warm brown eyes—the one thing that had skipped a generation was the inner daredevil. "With my daughter. This summer, they're planning to go skydiving—it will be her first time and his fifth."

"The closest I've ever come is parasailing in Sydney harbor. Remember that, Javi?" When he didn't answer, Lila nudged him with her elbow.

At that moment, Javier's text notification sounded. A quick glance at the screen settled his nerves.

Clear.

EV watched him intently without seeming to stare—it was an art she had perfected over the years when negotiating with art dealers. Whatever the message, it must have been good news, because the tension drained from him with a sigh, and he went back to being his charming self. The next hour passed in a haze of laughter, good wine, and better conversation.

"Perfect." Chloe said out loud, even though she was alone in the suite. An assortment of covered dishes adorned the small dinette table, and a bottle of champagne chilled on an adjacent stand. Deciding to take EV's advice and make sure Nate was in the best possible mood before admitting she had been less than honest with him, Chloe dimmed the lights and lit a few candles to set a romantic mood.

Nate was due to arrive any minute, so Chloe checked the gilded bathroom mirror one last time, making sure her hair and makeup were in place. A long, sapphire-colored skirt hugged her shapely hips, and a form-fitting sweater dipped low enough to display a white gold and sapphire pendant sparkling beneath her collarbone. Pedicured toes poked out from beneath the hem of the skirt, buffed and polished more scrupulously than usual, given that she went barefoot as much as possible back in the Pines.

Nate's gentle knock had Chloe skipping to the door, anxious both to see his handsome face, and to get the task at hand over with as quickly as she could. Though she wouldn't have believed it was possible, he looked even better than usual in a pair of black slacks and a white button-down shirt rolled up to his elbows. It was clear Nate had spent some time on his appearance: his usually-mussed hair had been trimmed and tamed into submission; his chiseled jawline accentuated in the absence of the scruff that normally resided there. Chloe's jaw hung open in appreciation until Nate let out a chuckle, slung his arms around her waist, and lifted her into a kiss.

"What happened to you?" she asked, as he released her gently back to the floor.

"What's that supposed to mean? Do I usually like some kind of hillbilly or something?" he teased, eyes crinkling at the edges as his wide grin belied the mock-serious tone of the question. "*Someone* left an appointment card in my room; I took the hint. Apparently, I had become too shaggy for this fancy place, so I visited the barber shop they've got hidden in the basement dungeon. Look, I even got what they call a MANicure." Sure enough, his nails had been cleaned and trimmed, and his palms were soft as silk where Chloe caressed them with her own fingers.

"I take it that's your first and last foray into a metro-sexual existence?"

"You can bet your ass, it is. Your mother has a lot of nerve, I can tell you that."

Chloe agreed, and, banishing all thoughts of her mother for at least the next couple of hours, led Nate to the table where she pulled the lids off all the plates. She had ordered an assortment of Irish dishes, including traditional Shepherd's pie, soda bread, and beef stew made with stout beer. She couldn't imagine Nate was missing American food; after all, what guy would complain about cuisine that included some type of alcohol in almost every dish?

They ate heartily, chatting about their day and enjoying each other's company away from the prying eyes of Lila, EV, and Dalton. When the last crumb of Irish cream cheesecake had been scraped from their plates, both their stomachs were so full, all they could do was flop down on the bed and allow digestion to take its course. Chloe figured this was as good a time as any to broach the subject.

"I have something I want to tell you. The thing is...there's something I haven't told you. It's not *bad*." She added, noting his small, concerned frown.

"Go on."

"Well...when I came back to the Pines, I spent a lot of time working on the house; decorating and remodeling and whatnot. And when I started job hunting, nothing nearby really appealed to me. You know I'm not exactly hurting for money, but I do like to keep busy." She picked at some lint on the spread so long he made an impatient hand gesture for her to continue.

"So...one day I was talking to Wesley about some of the freelance articles I wrote for a lifestyle magazine in New York. And he asked me to write something for the *Pine Cone*. I've been the author of 'Babble & Spin' ever since." She looked up into his eyes for the first time since beginning her speech, and was surprised to see amused relief in place of the irritation or anger she had expected.

"Jeez, Chlo, you had me thinking you were moonlighting as a topless dancer or something. And why are you so worked up about this?"

"Because I should have told you sooner. But I was sworn to secrecy. EV's the only one who knows, and that's only because she figured it out and then harassed me for two solid weeks before I confirmed. So...you're not mad?" she asked, hesitantly.

Nate gathered her face in his hands, kissed her lips, the tip of her nose, and her forehead before pulling her against his chest in a bone-crushing hug.

"Don't scare me like that again. I don't care that you write about gossip...wait...so that means it was *you* who started the *Inspector Hottie* nickname? You are so dead!" He flipped her onto her back, tickling her ribs and kissing the part of her neck that always made her giggle.

"No!" she cried out through teary-eyed laughter, attempting to swat him away. His torture lasted a few more seconds before, lips meeting hers again, their attention turned to other, more base desires.

Chapter 14

"Are you ready to talk?" Remy's voice woke Baylee from a light doze. He bent to pull the gag he'd fashioned from a silk tie from her mouth. Only a rasping sound escaped lips dry and cracked from a night spent in a bout of frustrated cursing him to a fate worse than death. If he thought he'd broken her—and she could tell by the triumphant lilt to his voice that he did—he was in for a surprise.

When he moved close to offer her a drink, she accepted the first swallow of water gratefully. "See, I told you I didn't want to hurt you. Just tell me where you hid the memory card, and as soon as I get it back, I'll let you go." The bottle bumped against her lips a second time. This mouthful she spat back at him. Rivulets ran down his face, which went hard right before he drew back an arm and slapped her once, then twice. Baylee's head rocked from side to side with the force.

"What were you doing in my room?" Remy demanded.

Cheek pulsing with pain from the sting of his hand, Baylee said, "They'll miss me when I don't show up for the photo shoot." Javier must already be scouring the castle for her. No way would he let her down. Javier was a rock.

Brandishing her cell phone, Remy smirked, "We'll just see about that." He let her watch him scroll through the increasingly frantic messages from Ross that had already come in. Fingers flashing, he typed a response, then switched off the phone and winged it into the stone wall behind her where it shattered into useless bits.

"No one even knows you're missing, and now they think you've been called away on a personal matter." He could be lying, but she didn't think so. "How do you know Lila's fiancé? His texts and messages sounded personal. Are you sleeping with him? Lila's a friend of mine."

He had the nerve to sound affronted at her perceived relationship with Javier.

Javier wasn't coming. At least not yet. That much

was clear. Baylee's breath hitched in her throat, while tears leaked down her still-smarting cheek. The moisture brought enough coolness to provide a little relief.

"Come on. I promise I won't hurt you. Once I have the memory card, I'll come back and let you go. It will be your word against mine, and who are they going to believe? What did he promise you to get you to cooperate? A cut of Lila's money? Or maybe you two *are* having an affair."

"I'm not sleeping with him, and I don't need Lila's money. You have a vile mind. Why would I tell you anything?"

"You'll tell me, or I'll see to it his little security business never gets another contract. I have connections, and I won't hesitate to use them." Fury puffed him up. "Tell me where the card is. You have my word that once the evidence is in my hand, I'll let you go. My little game is almost over, anyhow." Remy pulled his own phone out of his pocket. "Tell me now, or I'm going to make a call and bring Garritek down while you listen."

After everything Javier had done for her, Baylee couldn't let Vincent take anything more from him. She broke and told him where to find the card.

Where was everyone? Lila checked her watch for the tenth time. Javier was late, Baylee was late. Even Chloe and EV were late. Lila only planned to get married once in her life; everything had to be perfect. No one understood that but her. Frustration killed concern without mercy as she paced the length of the foyer where everyone should already have assembled.

Why had she let Javier talk her into this place? Sure, getting married in a castle sounded romantic enough, but the weather here this time of year was absolutely dismal. The sun was shining now, and, according to the photographer, this was the magic time of day when the light turned warm and rosy and flattering. Lila knew she looked good for her age, but she wasn't going to turn down anything that capitalized on her efforts. Who knew when the next bout of good weather might strike?

She was just pulling out her phone to call Chloe when Javier appeared at the top of the staircase, Chloe and EV right behind him. Lila's hand was still on her phone when it signaled a new text.

Unavoidably delayed. Sending my assistant to do the engagement photos.—Baylee.

"You're all late." Lila accused. Before she could

wind up a tirade, the elevator dinged and the doors opened. Ross, struggling with camera bags, tripods, a battery pack, and a stand topped by a large light, attempted to exit the elevator car. Chloe rushed down the last two steps and over to help. Her lengthy and eclectic job history included a stint as a photographer's assistant, so she juggled half the burden like a pro.

"Will Baylee be joining us?" Ross quailed at the sharp tone in Lila's voice.

"She had to leave for the day, that's all I know." He pulled a small, spiral-bound notepad from his shirt pocket, and flipped the pages. "Outdoor shots on the parapet and near the fountain." He cleared his throat, "Is that okay?"

Lila shot Chloe a look that boded ill for the hapless young man if someone didn't intervene, and by someone, Lila meant Chloe. Chloe took the hint.

"Come on, let's get this done before we lose the light. Ross, would you mind if I pitch in? I've got some experience." He could have said no, though it wouldn't have stopped her. Taking charge, Chloe handed a portion of the equipment off to EV, along with a murmured order to call Nate—something felt off to her about this whole scenario—and herded the group through the café and out the lower set of atrium doors, the fastest route to the fountain.

Two minutes of watching Ross fumble just getting the bags sorted turned Lila's face an unbecoming shade of mottled red. Chloe gave EV the elbow and whispered, "She's going to blow if I don't do something, and if her face gets any redder people will think this wedding took place in Tahiti. Talk her down while I sort this out."

Laying a hand on Ross's arm, Chloe pitched her voice low enough that with EV serving as a distraction, Lila couldn't overhear, and asked, "Have you ever done a shoot on your own before?"

Panic widened his eyes. "Does it show? All I've ever done are test shots."

"Would you mind if I take over?" Ross shook his head, relief pulling the tension from his body and steadying his hands.

"Okay." Chloe searched through through the equipment, chose a camera and lens. "Get me a gold reflector and start them out on the right side of the fountain. I'll take it from there."

"What's going on?" Nate approached EV. "Something wrong?"

"Baylee bailed on the shoot," she explained, noting the way his nostrils flared.

"And this required my presence because...?" He'd left Dalton waiting for confirmation to come in on a lead.

"You're probably here for damage control. Ross the assistant doesn't have the chops to handle it alone, so Chloe took over and that means her having to tell Lila what to do. I'm apparently not enough of an unknown quantity to ride herd on them, so you've been tapped for the job. And Chloe and I agree there's something off about Baylee's absence."

"Javier, tilt your head down just a little more. Mom, angle your chin slightly to the left." Barking orders and snapping the shutter, Chloe seemed in her element, and Nate was seeing a side of her he'd never observed before. Bossy but competent. He liked it. He liked it a lot. She put them through a series of poses that brought out a soft, vulnerable side of Lila he hadn't expected.

Ross, to his credit, was actually a very good assistant. He remained at Chloe's side, attentive to her every need, while EV stood behind the laptop to watch as the wireless transfer attachment on the camera delivered the images to a growing slideshow.

Glancing at the scrolling pictures, then back at Javier and Lila, Nate noted the difference between the strain on their faces and the soft, romantic images Chloe was able to capture. He also noted the tension that ran between her shoulders, and knew that if he went to her, the muscles would be bunched and knotted.

Through the atrium glass, a sea of interested faces watched the process from café tables. It felt like being on the wrong side of a fish bowl.

All business, Chloe gave Lila and Javier a short break from posing while she quickly scanned through the slideshow, deeming the images good enough to continue on to the parapet while the light held.

"Pack it up, Ross," she kept her tone even and professional, but Nate knew her well enough to know that this experience went deeper with her. While she would never have offered to perform this task, she relished the chance to create something timeless with her mother. Even if no one else saw it, he observed the tear of happiness that gathered in the corner of her eye when she saw the couple immortalized.

"Don't we still need the poses Hannah requested? I have the list she gave me." Ross asked, pulling a sheet of paper from his pocket.

Chloe stopped short and gaped at Ross for a moment before regaining her composure. "You spoke to Hannah? When?" She demanded.

"She caught up to me last night as I was leaving the dining room." He explained, bewildered by the Chloe's sudden coldness toward the wedding coordinator. She seemed nice enough to him; though that could have had something to do with the flirtatious nature of their conversation.

"Hannah Frank is not involved in this wedding, and I'd recommend you don't breathe her name around my mother. I guess Baylee didn't mention that part to you." She softened at his obvious distress. "Don't worry about it. Just don't give her copies of any of the images or there'll be hell to pay."

Ross nodded in assent, and moved to clear up the equipment. With Nate and EV lending a hand, he had everything broken down and ready to move in a matter of minutes. Back in the lobby, Dalton exited the elevator at the same time the group trooped toward the courtyard access doors leading to narrow stairs that granted access to the parapets. Catching Nate's eye, Dalton's shoulders lifted slightly—he shook his head.

"Let me help you with that," Javier reached for one of the heavy bags. Chloe relinquished it willingly.

"Do you have the key card for Baylee's room, Ross?" Javier wasn't the only one concerned about Baylee. EV wanted the chance to look around.

"Yes, ma'am. But you all don't have to help; it's my job." Ross reached for the softbox lamp EV carried, but snatched his hand back when he caught the stern expression on her face.

EV patted him on the shoulder, "Lead the way." Her tone brooked no refusal, and, taking the elevator for the sake of convenience, they all trooped to Baylee's door.

"You can just leave everything here." Ross didn't want to cause inconvenience, or worse, have Baylee catch him letting her clients play pack mule. Not to mention the hot water he would be in for bringing half a dozen people into her room uninvited.

"Open the door. We won't let you get into trouble." EV softened her voice, but made no move to put down her burden, nor did anyone else. Ross caved easily; he didn't have the guts to argue.

Taking a deep breath, Ross ran the card through the reader, pushed open the door, then led the way to the closet area where they helped him stow everything away neatly. The first thing EV noticed was a handbag lying on the bed. "How likely is it that Baylee left for the day without taking this?" She strode over to check for a wallet, and finding one, brandished it in the air.

"I have a bad feeling about this," Javier shook his head. "Baylee would not leave Ross alone to do her work. Something must have happened to her." And he had a pretty good idea what. "We need to call the authorities." His face lost enough color that the olive of his skin turned a sallow yellow-green.

"In the states, we can't investigate until someone has been missing at least 48 hours. It's probably the same here. More often than not, the missing person turns up with a perfectly valid reason for their absence. It can't hurt, though, to ask a few questions."

"We must do everything we can to find her." His voice rising, Javier said, "If she never made it back from...she could be in danger."

Back in the elevator, EV addressed Javier, "Made it back from where? Do you know something you'd like to share with the rest of us?" Was Javier really the thief Chloe suspected him of being, and had he dragged his sister-in-law into something over her head? EV glanced at Lila, whose face showed concern, but not suspicion, as she ran a soothing hand up and down his arm. If there was something more to the story with Baylee and Javier, Lila knew what it was. Or, she thought she did. When EV opened her mouth to question him further, Lila shot her a pleading look with a tiny shake of her head. Reluctantly, EV let it go. For now.

Lila said, "Let me be the one to talk to Antoine; he's more likely to spill what he knows to me than to you, Nate." A hint of regret colored her tone.

"Why? Because you fed him some line of bull about me so he would give me a room as far away from Chloe's as he could find?"

"Maybe."

"Yeah, I thought so. He gives me a dirty look every time he sets eyes on me. What exactly did you tell him?"

Lila waved a dismissive hand, "Nothing really bad, I think he jumped to conclusions."

"If he was jumping, you supplied the pogo stick," Chloe tossed the comment back over her shoulder, along with an attempt at a quelling glare for EV who, with Dalton, occupied the space behind Lila and Javier. Both had snickered at her comment. "If you wanted time with me for yourself, Mother, all you had to do was say so. I've missed you, too."

The elevator dinged and shuddered to a stop. Lila approached Antoine while the others hung back.

When asked if he had seen Baylee leave the castle that afternoon, Antoine shook his head emphatically. Not only had Baylee not been one of those in line for the daily shuttle into the village, she had not passed through the foyer or lobby area all day. All other exits led to walled enclosures and courtyards. Anyone leaving would have to pass Antoine or his night time counterpart, or exit through one of the fire exits, which would set off an alarm. No alarm meant Baylee was still in the castle.

Chapter 15

Silence enveloped the six people packed into the elevator like a bunch of nervous sardines; each mind wondering where Baylee could be. "Let's order some room service and regroup. If we're going to get to the bottom of this, we need sustenance and a plan." Nate shot a questioning look at Lila, who he pegged as the most likely to object. She merely nodded in assent. At this point, she was more than happy to keep a trained police officer nearby, and sticking together seemed like the safest option.

Chloe's head fell against Nate's chest, the quiet thumping of his heart lulling her into a dreamlike state. A low rumble in her belly at Nate's mention of food reminded her that she hadn't eaten yet today. People disappearing out of thin air didn't exactly whet the appetite. Breadsticks with legs, a smiling cartoon chicken cutlet, and a head of romaine lettuce wearing a sombrero danced across the backs of her eyelids. A sharp ding, signaling they had arrived on their floor broke Chloe from her trance.

"I miss real food. Want to cook. Miss my kitchen." She murmured quietly to Nate, who couldn't help nodding in agreement. Homesickness—an emotion that Chloe, having never stayed in one place long enough to consider it home—hit her hard in the face. *So this is what that feels like. Maybe I can click my heels together three times and forget about this whole mess.*

Chloe's key card was at the ready, and when she swiped to open the door, everyone filed in behind her. A strangled cry escaped her lips as she looked around the room. Clothing spilled out of open drawers; the bed was stripped, the mattress askew as if someone had searched beneath it; every piece of luggage overturned. Several lacy undergarments littered the floor, but embarrassment wasn't a luxury Chloe could afford right now—her room had been ransacked.

Nate raised an arm, gently pushing everyone back into the hallway. "Dalton, stay here and guard the exits. I'll clear the suites; make sure this son of a bitch isn't still skulking around." He looked around, pulled an umbrella from the stand inside the door, and made a couple of practice lunges with it. If the situation were different, Chloe might have giggled out loud at the sight of her hunky boyfriend brandishing an umbrella sword.

"Better than nothing." Nate shrugged, then disappeared inside. After the longest three minutes of Chloe's life, he emerged from the door to EV's portion of the suite. "All clear. Whoever it was seemed to be focused on Chloe's room, but EV's was searched as well. Lila, the door to your room was locked, so I'm assuming it hasn't been touched. I'll call in security, and then you two need to check all of your belongings and see if anything is missing."

Everyone followed Nate's instructions; fear, anxiety, and concern coloring all six faces. Dalton followed EV into her room; Javier ordered Lila to wait while he checked theirs, just in case Nate was wrong about it not having been accessible. When they were alone, Nate pulled Chloe close and held on tight. "I'm not letting you out of my sight until I know you're safe."

"Mother will love that." Chloe hid fear and uncertainty behind a wall of humor. It was a short wall, though, and easily breached. "I feel violated." Nate squeezed her even tighter. Until this business with Baylee and the break in, Nate thought Chloe's suspicion of Javier to be based on concern for Lila. Watching more critically now, he was sure the man had a stake in what was happening, and the time for withholding information was just about over.

A room away, Dalton said, "EV, This goes beyond catching Remy. Screw him; it's not worth your safety. If he sees us together, that's just too bad. He's got something to do with this, I can feel it in my bones." Dalton had waited until they were alone in EV's room to pull her close, but there was no trace of hesitation in the action.

EV leaned into his embrace and spoke her mind. He had expected no less. "We can't throw away all we've worked for over this. This isn't the first room to be broken into, and nobody has gotten hurt so far. Let's not overreact. If we blow our cover now, we'll never find out why he's terrorizing Ponderosa Pines. I want to put this to rest once and for all."

Dalton sighed. Leave it to EV to put her own safety on the back burner. "Let's talk to Nate and Chloe; figure out how we're going to handle this." Dalton would humor EV, but in the end, nothing— not even her iron will—would stop him from protecting her.

"You'll understand, I went through proper channels on this. Hotel management is contacting the security staff. They'll be able to analyze how the room was accessed, and they'll review the video footage of the hallway outside. It's all going to take some time. They requested that we check if anything was missing—as if that's not the first thing any sane person would do in this situation. When I said we already had, and everything was accounted for, I got the impression that our priority level dropped significantly. Now that we've put in an official complaint, you can probably facilitate things on that front, Javier." Nate explained, once everyone had reassembled in Chloe's room. He ran his hands through his hair; it didn't have the usual effect, given his new, shorter style.

"I'll handle this; none of you need to worry. Several guests have complained about missing items lately, and in each case, the objects were found right away." Javier paced around the room, lost in thought. "People misplace things all the time, but when they go to a hotel, the first assumption is that someone—usually the housekeeping staff—is stealing. Though, none of the reports lately have included an actual security breach, so maybe this has to do with Baylee's disappearance." Storm clouds gathered in his eyes before he schooled his features again.

"How could someone get in here without a key?" Nate asked.

"They would have to hack into the security mainframe, and either activate a new key card or remotely unlock the door. The second option would require more than one person; someone to hit the switch, and someone to open the door. Seems like an awful lot of trouble considering nothing is missing." Javier explained. "Come to think of it, are we sure all the room keys are accounted for?"

EV searched her pockets, wallet, and the small backpack she most often carried instead of a handbag. Chloe's key card was on the console table near the door, right where she had dropped it when they walked in. Lila and Javier were able to produce their own within moments. A strangled "damn it all" echoed from EV's room, where she had retreated in search of the last key.

"It's my fault." She moaned. "It's not in my bag, or any of my pockets. My key is missing."

"When was the last time you know you had it?" Javier questioned.

"It's been a couple of days." Her face screwed up

while she accessed her memory, "Maybe more. I haven't left the room without Chloe by my side except for last night, and when we came back, I went in through the connecting door from Lila's room. They got in with my key, and then it was easy to get to Chloe's things. I'm so sorry." She whispered.

A chorus of reassurances rang out as Dalton kneaded her shoulders in an attempt to soothe her nerves. Chloe noticed, even through the haze of worry in which she was currently mired, that EV did not shrug away from Dalton's touch as she had in the past.

"They're right; it's not your fault. If someone wanted to get in here this badly, they would have found another way." Javier reassured EV before turning his attention back to Lila. "Are you going to be okay, love?" He asked at her visible distress.

She didn't answer. In fact, she couldn't bring herself to say anything at all. Instead, she stood stock-still, hands clenched at her sides, white rage spreading through her entire body. The others watched as almost visible emotion roiled off her. Chloe shrank back, closed her eyes, and waited for the diatribe to begin.

"There will be hell to pay if this doesn't get

resolved in a timely manner! This is supposed to be the happiest time of my life, and it's turning into a nightmare! You're all distracted; my photographer—and friend—is missing; my family is being threatened; and I've got the wedding planner from Hades following me around like a tail, trying to satisfy my every desire! Now my suite has been broken into, my daughter's room has been ransacked, and security is going to try to put me on the back burner? I. Don't. Bloody. Think. So. I can't handle worrying about all of you while also pulling off a spectacular event. This isn't the time. Maybe we should postpone the wedding."

She shot a helpless look at Javier, then continued to stomp around the room, stuffing articles of clothing back into drawers, straightening pillows, and muttering to herself. Nobody spoke, until finally, she collapsed into Chloe's waiting arms. As Lila sobbed into her daughter's shoulder, Chloe's gaze met Javier's. Concern and helplessness etched into the lines on his face; his eyes flicked over to the door, and Chloe nodded slightly. Lila needed to get some air; clear her head before going off on the hotel staff.

"That's not an option. We'll get this resolved, and then we're getting married." Javier's voice hardened momentarily, then softened as he gazed at Lila's contorted expression. "Come on, darling, let's take a walk. Then we can go have a little chat with hotel management and take a look at that security footage. Whether they want me to or not." He suggested. Lila kissed Chloe on the cheek, smiled weakly at the rest of the group, and followed him out the door without another word.

"Well, it's not hard to see where you got your penchant for ranting, Chlo." EV chuckled lightly, attempting to inject some humor into the room. Nate's eyebrow twitched, and Chloe let a bubble of nervous laughter escape her lips.

Dalton was the first to speak what had been weighing on everyone's minds. "Does it seem to you all like trouble just keeps popping up whenever Remy Vincent is involved? Or am I paranoid because I want to see the bastard behind bars, where he belongs?"

"I don't think you're wrong." EV reassured him. "But we've been over and over this before, and can't figure out what his motive would be. It's a possibility, but if it *was* him, he clearly didn't find what he was looking for. Nothing is missing, and everything we brought with us is in these rooms. What could he possibly be looking for?"

"Let's get real, here. It's obvious to me that Javier is to blame." Chloe interjected. "My instincts are screaming that he's hiding something. Isn't it convenient that his and my mother's suite wasn't touched—and that he has intimate knowledge of what it would take to break in? Not to mention that he has access to the security footage? We know he has an accomplice; we heard him talking on the phone. This could be the break in he was talking about."

"Why would he break into a suite that's attached to his own room, and then take nothing? It makes no sense. He could have left the door unlocked and come in here any time, leaving no trace. Why would he steal EV's room key? It didn't sound like he was planning on stealing a key; it sounded like he was planning on screwing with the system to gain access that way. And what could he possibly want?" Nate asked. "If you think it through, you'll agree." He gave her a minute to consider and watched as she visibly calmed, then reconsidered.

Chloe looked at each of them in turn. "This isn't a coincidence; it wasn't random. This person was looking for something specific. I agree that Javier had access to our room without sneaking around, and I don't think he would make his presence known. Plus,

I saw his face when we walked in here; if he wasn't truly surprised, he deserves an Oscar nod. But I'm still not convinced of his complete innocence. What better way to cover your tracks than by having your own suite broken into? Maybe it's a distraction technique, so when the real theft happens security will assume it's just another false alarm."

Nate shook his head. "I'm not sure. We're missing something. Maybe we're looking at it from the wrong angle."

"Well, I, for one, think we should take advantage of this opportunity. Javier and Lila are distracted, and Chloe isn't going to let him off the hook until we're sure about what he's hiding. We have no access to Remy's room, but we do have access to Javier's. See where I'm going with this?" They all nodded agreement with EV's suggestion.

"Let's do it."

Dalton nudged open the door to the hallway and stayed close to listen in case Javier and Lila circled back to the suite unexpectedly, while EV, Nate, and Chloe picked carefully through Javier's belongings. If he was, indeed, planning on ripping Lila off, maybe this was a preemptive strike designed to throw suspicion onto some unknown party.

"Nothing here, just clothes. This guy is seriously organized; even his underpants are perfectly folded. I've never seen such an OCD suitcase." EV unzipped a garment bag next, discovering nothing but an exquisite suit accompanied by a perfectly accented tie and pocket square matching Lila's designer wedding gown.

Chloe rifled through the bedside tables, but quickly abandoned the empty drawers; Javier hadn't bothered to unpack. She checked the matching dresser with no luck.

"Hey, I think I found something!"

Around the corner toward where the corridor dead-ended, Remy waited while Dalton stood outside the door like a palace guard. He'd have to go back inside eventually and there was no reason for him to come this direction, but if there was one thing Remy Vincent loved, it was instant gratification. Waiting for anything he really wanted chafed at him like ants crawling over his skin. Now he was stuck on the wrong end of the hallway; to get back to his room, he needed to pass the spot where Dalton stood.

He pulled his head back. Stupid Burnsoll. No sense of personal awareness at all. Remy knew he would feel eyes on him if someone watched him the way he was watching Dalton now. Must make one lousy cop.

"I'll take that." Dalton's voice echoed toward Remy, who risked another look just in time to see a member of the staff hand over what Remy had come here to find: a carefully wrapped sheaf of dry cleaning. Nostrils flaring, Remy stepped back to wait until the hallway was clear. This was not turning out to be his day. Not at all.

Nate bent over a brown leather satchel, running a finger over a set of initials tooled into the surface. "JR. Javier Rosales. This is definitely his, and it looks well-used. It's something he's carried for a long time. Perfect place to keep valuables." Nate opened the bag and began to rifle through the contents while the others watched. Dalton stepped away from his post by the door to get a closer look.

A tattered photograph fluttered to the floor and landed face down. EV picked it up and read aloud what was written in script across the back. "Javier Rosales and Tomas Delarosa. 1995." She turned the photo over and stared into the face of a thirty-something Javier, his arm resting on the shoulder of another tanned, good-looking man who must have been in his early twenties.

"You've got to be kidding me." Nate and Dalton shared an incredulous look; this wasn't the first time they had heard the name Tomas Delarosa. "What are the odds?" The two men shared a look as something clicked.

"Will you *please* tell me what the hell is going on here?" Chloe screeched, her nerves shot and her patience reaching its end.

"Tomas Delarosa was one of the names we found

in connection with Remy Vincent. I think you might have been right all along, Chloe. If Javier is mixed up with Remy, your mother is in big trouble."

The sound of throat clearing behind them interrupted the series of open mouth looks being exchanged. As one, the four of them whirled guiltily.

Javier stood in the doorway blocking Lila from the room. The photo in Chloe's hand and the look on her face told him it was time to come clean. With everyone. His hand speared through his hair in an uncharacteristic gesture, leaving it ruffled and messy. Behind him, Lila gave a nudge, then stood on tiptoe to peer around him in order to see what was holding him up.

Grudgingly, Javier moved into the room. "That's my brother Tomas." He reached out to gently take the photo from Chloe's hand. "Come, Lila, sit here with me. I need to tell you some things." Deep regret colored the words. Not regret for having to finally tell the whole story, but for keeping any of it from her to begin with. She knew most, but not all.

"A year and a half ago, my brother, Tomas, was the victim of identity theft. In the computer age, this is a common occurrence all over the world. At first, we assumed that freezing his accounts and getting new documents would be enough to protect him. But it was not. The thief created an elaborate network of stolen identities, while leaving a false trail of evidence that pointed straight to my brother. I'm sure you all know by now that the actual culprit was Remy Vincent."

"I don't understand, the name we found in connection with Remy was Tomas Delarosa. Not Tomas Rosales." Scorn was rife in the words Chloe flung at him and she noted the frown that her words brought to Lila's face. Apparently, Javier had not told her mother the entire story.

"Tomas is my stair brother—" he paused to think, "step is the term, I believe. My mother remarried after my father died. Tomas was very young. His father and my mother had both lost their first loves and, together, they found solace, family."

Gently grasping Lila's hand, Javier continued. The prospect of speaking this next part out loud had his heart thumping in his chest. He stood to lose her if she couldn't forgive him for what he had done.

"When the police came to arrest my brother, I vowed to him that I would do everything in my power to clear his name. Even now that more evidence has come to light, he has not been fully exonerated. Remy Vincent cost Tomas everything. He spent his savings to mount a defense, then he had to leave our business to keep it from going under due to the strain on his reputation. We cut all ties to, and then buried his connection with Garritek to preserve our livelihood."

Lila squeezed his hand. Javier had told her about Tomas, though not in great detail, and certainly not that Remy had been the man behind the frame job his brother had been caught in.

"Six months ago, Tomas broke under the strain. He walked away from his family," Javier's voice sounded choked with emotion. "He tried to kill himself. It was only through God's mercy that I found him in time." He paused for a long minute to pull himself together. "I vowed that I would clear his name, no matter the price."

So far, Lila had not pulled away. Now he would say the words that might cost him his future with her.

"I cashed in favors with everyone I knew from my security work. Private investigators, Interpol—I even hired a hacker—and followed the trail to Remy, but there was never enough evidence for a warrant. I investigated every connection I could find—

including EV and you, Lila." He turned to her. "Please don't hate me. When I found you, it was under the guise of learning more about Vincent. I planned to shamelessly exploit the connection if there was any way you could lead me to him. If I had known that you would turn out to be the love of my life, I'm not sure I would have done anything differently. In fact, if I had known the trail would lead me to you, the only thing I would alter is that I would have put my feet on it earlier. Every day of my life without you in it was a paler version. Say you'll forgive me."

Javier's eyes searched Lila's for signs of recrimination. If she turned away from him now, his world would become a bleak, colorless place.

At that point, Chloe broke in, "I knew you had an ulterior motive. I just expected it to be money, not revenge."

He turned toward Chloe, and when she saw the naked fear written on his face, now pale and grave, she relented. "Give him a break, Mom; takes a pretty decent guy to go to such lengths to protect his family. You could do a lot worse. Besides, he's growing on me." Javier gave her a half smile and a nod of thanks.

"She's right." EV tossed in her two cent's worth before Nate spoke up.

"We should get out of here," he said, "and give them some privacy."

"No. Stay right here." Lila finally spoke. "There's nothing to forgive. You could have told me before, and it would have made no difference." She cupped his cheek in her hand, "I don't care what your motives were for finding me, I'm just glad that you did." Her kiss was gentle, a soothing balm to his soul.

"Well, it took him more than fifty years, but it looks like Remy finally did something right." EV's humorous observation broke the tension. She ran through the Ponderosa Pines part of the story quickly, bringing Javier up to speed. "Now can we please make a plan for dealing with the piece of slime? Or do the two of you need to get a room?"

Color returned to Javier's face and he could take a full breath without worrying that his world was about to come crashing down; his mind cleared.

"We have a room, but I think we can hold out while we discuss the business at hand. With our combined evidence and testimony, we might just be able to nail him to the wall." Javier couldn't stop grinning though the look in his eyes was fierce.

"Assuming Vincent had an opportunity to lift

EV's key card, it had to have been him who went through Chloe's things."

"What about the other incidents we've been hearing about?" Dalton questioned.

"Non-issues." Javier said, "a misplaced piece of jewelry that turned up later—money *borrowed* by a teenager from his father's wallet. Nothing of consequence. The glitch in the system that caused safe doors to reprogram inaccurately was down to one of the security technician's error. This is the only genuine break in, and assuming it was Vincent, the only question is: what was he looking for?"

"All of that makes perfect sense," Nate said thoughtfully, "it comes down to why he went rifling through Chloe's things? You're sure nothing is missing, Chlo?"

"Not that I can see."

Javier suddenly lost all the color his face had regained only moments before. "Baylee."

"Baylee?" Lila said.

"I've one more story to tell." Javier strode across the room where he stood, facing out the balcony doors with his back to the others who stood waiting for his next revelation. "Now that you know about Tomas, you'll have realized Baylee is his wife. We made arrangements to access the safe in his room in our search for evidence."

"HA! That explains the conversation Nate and I overheard," Chloe's outburst caused Javier to turn in surprise.

"Now I can see why you've been suspicious of me for so long. In any case, no one has seen Baylee since she left to search his room."

EV's voice dripped ice, "And you're only telling us this now?"

"I received a text from her later with the all clear message, and then Ross said she had contacted him, so I assumed she had other reasons for not wanting to be with people right now; that she was dealing with distress over coming up empty yet again."

"What does that have to do with Remy breaking into my room?" Chloe didn't see the connection.

"If she was in trouble, Baylee would come straight to me, so it makes perfect sense that she might have made her way back here. And yet, she's still missing. Perhaps she was intercepted by Vincent. You must help me find her."

Chapter 17

Nate laid a sheet of paper out on the table. His hands flew across the pristine whiteness to sketch a quick diagram of the castle's layout between Remy's room and Lila's suite. "Stashing her in his own room would be risky."

"Lacking a key card, he wouldn't have had access to a vacant room, even if he could find one," Javier agreed.

"That leaves storage areas and the portion of the castle that hasn't yet been renovated." Nate looked up to see nods of agreement. "He'd have to get her out of sight quickly, which means he would have gone for the nearest area to where he caught her. Dragging a resisting woman through populated corridors would be stupid."

"This is all my fault." Javier paced the room like a caged animal. "I shouldn't have let her get involved. We thought if we had some evidence to show the authorities—any kind of proof—they would have to take action."

"We'll find her." Nate bit the words out.

EV stood behind Nate to look over his shoulder. "Assuming she made it back to here," EV pointed to the area that corresponded with her own room, then glanced at the exterior photos on the castle brochure spread open near Nate's drawing, "there's an unused turret section there."

Spinning the drawing to face him, Dalton pointed toward the south wing, "And an entire area blocked off over here. So we concentrate on this section? How did he get her past the security cameras?"

"I can answer that, I had the cameras along her route on a loop. Once Baylee was clear, she was supposed to text me so I could put them back on live feed. I waited an extra five minutes in case she'd gotten held up. By then, it was too late."

"Is there anywhere between his room and ours where another camera may have picked up something?" EV ran her finger along the most direct route between Remy's room and her own. "Be worth checking the videos to see if he shows up. Do the cameras record sound?"

Javier turned pale and slumped heavily onto a

chair. "Yes, of course. I should have thought to check immediately. The footage would still be in the system." He ran a hand over a day's growth of whiskers; the perfectly pressed and groomed man was slowly devolving into a haggard, sleep-deprived one. Baylee was family, or close enough to it that he had let worry overrule common sense. "I'll go right now."

"I'll come with you." Lila insisted, "two sets of eyes and ears are better than one." He squeezed her hand as the two headed for the door to be stopped by a question from Chloe.

"Is it going to be enough? What she found, I mean." Chloe fidgeted with her hair; twirling it around a finger absentmindedly. "It would have to be, right? Otherwise, what reason would he have had to detain her."

"Probably would have been." The glance Nate cast at Javier was filled with pique. "If her bout of B&E hadn't rendered the evidence useless by being obtained without a warrant."

"I was trying to help. I had no idea anyone was actively pursuing Vincent. I'm sorry."

Knowing that Baylee had put herself in danger for nothing took even more of a toll on Javier. Head down, and, shoulders slumped with defeat, he led Lila out the door to see if there was anything he could do to help salvage the situation.

"If we can't count on Baylee's evidence, it's back to plan A. EV, are you sure you want to go through with it?" Dalton laid a hand on her shoulder giving it a gentle squeeze.

"If I get him to confess, can we put him behind bars?"

"Fraud and identity theft carry a fifteen year maximum in the states—and we can prove multiple counts. Now that we know his crimes were not confined just to the U.S., I'll need to contact Interpol. Even without Evan being alive to testify, I think we can add extortion to the list—and kidnapping. He'll have good lawyers, but he'll do time."

"What about Baylee and Javier?" Chloe asked. "I assume there will be repercussions."

Nate's shoulders lifted. "That will depend on whatever the evidence shows. It will be up to the local authorities to pursue. It was a foolhardy thing to do."

"What would you have done in his position?" Chloe demanded. Now that she'd accepted him as family, she would defend Javier to the bitter end.

Nate's sheepish grin was enough of an answer, but he clarified anyway. "I'd have done the same." His face firmed. "But, we can't cover this up, or ignore the facts. Even with extenuating circumstances, he broke the law. Whatever happens, it's out of our hands."

The stage was set, the players ready to take their places. Javier, Lila, and Chloe would search for Baylee while Nate, Dalton, and EV handled Remy—keeping him away from Baylee and, with any luck, extracting a confession from him at the same time.

There was one more thing EV needed to do before it was time to act. Unable to sit still with nervous energy coursing through her veins, her feet carried her back and forth across seating area in Lila's suite.

"Nate, I..."

"You're not backing out on me are you, EV?" Looking up from the notes he was making on his laptop, Nate took in the set lines of her face, the stiff shoulders, and jumped to conclusions.

"Of course not." EV crossed the small space, sliding into the chair next to him. One way or another, she needed to get Remy back to the suite so this could all go down in a private setting. On the other side of the door connecting Chloe's bedroom to Lila's suite, Nate would be waiting to ensure her safety once she had Remy in there. For Dalton, being half a castle away, even while she was amid the crowded dining room wasn't good enough. Disguised by a hat pulled low over his face, a pair of thick glasses, and enhanced with makeup applied by Chloe's skilled hand, he would be sitting several tables away from where EV and Remy were to meet.

"It's just that there's something you need to know about Remy and me before I can go through with this. Something that's bound to come up, and I'd rather you hear it now than be surprised by it later." EV spoke quietly, but with heavy intent. Nate gave her his full attention.

Each telling of the story of her final days with Remy became easier. By the cold fury that leapt into Nate's eyes, EV could tell Chloe had kept her secret—this was the first Nate had heard of her history. He called Remy a spate of names that were vicious enough to slap an admiring grin on EV's face, and release the tension she held inside. "Now that we've gotten that out of the way, how do you want me to play this?" Nate's indignation on her behalf had lightened her mood considerably.

"Javier spent some time with the head of security for the castle. The staff here uses handheld communication devices, so it wasn't that hard for the two of them to rig up a couple of wired microphones and transmitters. We can follow your conversation with Remy in real time." Nate held up a smallish piece of electronic equipment. "I'll be on the other end, recording everything." He spun the laptop so she could see the program open and ready.

"I'll be wearing the same gear and sitting behind Remy—far enough where he won't hear me, but close enough so you can see me. I won't let you out of my sight," Dalton assured her.

"Javi and his team have a set of handheld radios, which I will also be monitoring, but you'll only be able to hear Dalton or me through the ear piece. Your hair covers your ears, so Remy won't see it, and we'll tape everything down so you won't have to worry about it coming dislodged when you move. I'll be here to guide you, but we're relying on you to pull a confession out of him." Nate patted her shoulder awkwardly, then turned back to his typing.

"Now, Dalton will do the honors of getting you fitted out with the equipment." Nate's face burned red at the thought of touching EV intimately enough to run the wires and tape them where they would stay concealed by her clothing. His embarrassment brought a smile to her face.

Gentle on her skin, Dalton's hands sent tingles of electricity shivering across it when he tucked the thin, black strand into her bra. His eyes lifted to hers, held there for a moment to speak promises for their future when this was over. He leaned in to whisper, "I believe in you."

Pulling her eyes away with difficulty, EV checked her watch. Five minutes and counting before she had to leave in order to meet Remy in the café; her heart kicked in her chest. Never before had the weight of caring for her town—for Ponderosa Pines and every soul who lived there—pressed so heavily on her shoulders. Concern for Baylee's safety only added to the burden. If she couldn't figure out a way to lead Remy into confessing his reason for targeting her town and committing crimes in the process, he would feel free to continue on with his vendetta.

More, she had to time this right in order to give Lila, Chloe, and Javier a chance to find Baylee in case she failed. If Remy decided they were on to him, there was no telling what he might do to Javi's sister-in-law before they could stop him. Or what he might have already done to her, which was EV's biggest fear. She was going on the assumption that, even after all this time, she was at the heart of his motive. If Baylee got hurt because of her, EV would never forgive herself.

A second laptop sat on the table—this one Dalton's—linked to Javier's, which currently displayed the castle's security camera feed. Feeling like a guillotine hovered above her neck, EV watched Remy leave his room. Once upon a time, this man had been the boy who she loved with her whole heart. Looking at him now, all evidence of that boy seemed tarnished and jaded—and she mourned their loss even as she burned with fury at everything he had done. The pedestal she had set him on at fourteen had obviously been formed from wet sand, tempered by time—not into cement, but into a crumbling foundation that toppled him to the ground. The time for mercy was long past. She reached for Dalton's hand; let his strength course through her one last time before he left the room to find his place in the café.

Chapter 18

In the cramped security room, Javier slammed his fist down on the table, jarring the state-of-the-art laptop resting there. He'd split the display into four separate video inputs: one replaying security footage of the hallway outside Baylee's suite, one of the hallway outside Lila's, and a third showing the perspective from the only camera close enough to have caught any extraneous images at the time of Baylee's disappearance.

The final quadrant—the camera nearest Remy's room—played in reverse, from now to the time of Baylee's disappearance, so Javier could watch his movements during the period in question. "There, he's headed in that direction after leaving his room three separate times in the last 24 hours." Javier looked hopeful as he watched Remy skulk out of his room in the opposite direction of the bank of elevators that would have been the easiest way to get to the main section of the castle.

"So what now?" Lila asked. "Where does that course take him?"

"To the west wing, and to the stairs leading down the level our rooms are on."

Javier was already clicking furiously between files on the main security console, his sharp eyes scanning between several sets of blueprints and security plans, searching for the most likely place Remy would have stashed Baylee. Chloe and Lila exchanged a nervous glance; this was their best chance to find Javier's sister-in-law. With Nate and Dalton monitoring EV's attempt to wheedle a confession out of Remy, they had a clear shot at a rescue, and would receive a heads-up if Remy tried to break away.

"There are several unmonitored areas he could access once he entered the turret, depending on whether he went up or down. Some are unusable; others are pending construction, so there's nothing there to steal, which is why we didn't install cameras. When we get there, we can split up and cover more ground. If this doesn't work, we're going to have to trust EV to pry the information from him, or trail him until he leads us to her. I'd rather not go there; he's unpredictable and reckless, and I don't want anyone getting hurt."

Lila wrapped a protective arm around Chloe's shoulders while they both remained silent and allowed Javier to come up with a plan of attack. Minutes later, he whipped three sheets of paper off the portable printer resting in the far corner of the room and handed them each a map. "He could have gone up or down; I'll take the bottom floor and work my way up. You two start at the top and work your way down; we'll meet in the middle. We'll stay in contact with these," He passed Chloe a hand-held radio. "This one is set to communicate only with mine, while I will be able to monitor both yours and the same frequency Nate, Dalton, and EV are using. This way, we can stay in constant contact in the event that EV's plan goes south and Remy tries to make off in this direction. You'll need to push this button to talk, and this is the volume. Call me with your progress; I will do the same, and I'll relay to Nate when we find her. And we will find her. Be quick and be safe."

Javier kissed Lila quickly and enveloped both mother and daughter in a tight hug.

"You take the left side, I'll take the right." Lila

nodded at Chloe's suggestion, took a deep breath and turned the handle of the first door. A once-elegant, now dust-covered sleeping area lay behind the entrance. Light spattered across the room through heavy brocade draperies ravaged by time and a particularly hungry eclipse of moths. No disturbance in the thick layer of dust and dirt caking the floor told Lila this room hadn't been entered recently, but she stepped a boot-clad foot inside and searched the adjoining powder room and closet anyway.

Halfway down the hallway, Chloe let out a frustrated grunt. "I really don't think he's been on this floor. Nothing has been touched here in about a hundred years. It seems like he'd want to be as close as possible to wherever he's keeping her, which means we're all starting in the wrong place."

"I think you're right." Lila crouched down, cocked her head to the side, and peered at the stone floor spreading down the rest of the hallway. "There are no footprints anywhere. Just more dust. Let's go downstairs. I think we'll have better luck there."

Chloe keyed up the radio, "No one's been up here for a very long time. We're moving down a level."

In response, she heard a short burst of static, then Javier's voice, "Noted."

Javier, near upon the same conclusion Lila and Chloe had drawn, was making his way through the last of the first floor rooms when the hallway's connecting door creaked open. Quick as a cat, he assembled himself into a casual stance, silenced the two-way radio, and ambled toward the exit closest the main section of the castle.

From around the corner peeked the curious face of none other than Hannah Frank. Her searching gaze spoke volumes; clearly, the relentless woman had followed him, hoping to ferret out some nugget of useful information. Several thoughts buzzed through Javier's mind: how much did she know? How long had she been following him? Was she connected to Remy, or just an intolerable snoop?

"Hello, Javier." She greeted him brightly, as if a chance meeting in a deserted castle hallway was completely normal. "Where is our blushing bride?" Looking past him, her expression turned to one of defeat when she realized Lila was nowhere to be seen. *Intolerable snoop, it is.*

Javier sighed heavily, his face darkening to convey irritation—he didn't have time for this, and had hit his limit with the pestering woman. Even as they spoke, Chloe or Lila could be trying to contact him via the two-way radio.

"She's down in the salon, I think, or maybe she said she was going to take a steam." Javier pasted on a fake smile and directed Hannah to the furthest reaches of the castle, hoping she'd take the bait and scurry off on the misguided mission.

The unexpected jangle of his cell phone nearly had him jumping out of his own skin. "Sorry, Hannah, but I have to take this." He barked. Without absorbing the hard edge to his words, she was already headed back toward the exit with a hopeful smile on her face.

"Are you alright?" Lila's voice rang clear with concern. "Why aren't you answering on the radio?"

"That damnable Hannah woman was tailing me, looking for you. I think I've dispatched her for the time being." Javier cracked the door she had disappeared through, making sure he was fully in the clear, then broke into a sprint in the other direction.

"We're close; she's got to be in one of these rooms. Someone has been through here lately; we can see footprints going in and out. Call Antoine; he's going to want to see this, and we need to make sure a staff member can attest to her condition."

"On my way." Elation coursed through Javier's veins; for a moment, he didn't care what happened to Remy Vincent, as long as Baylee was all right. Still, he felt a responsibility to take the bastard down. It was clear Remy was getting desperate, and that meant it was only a matter of time before someone else got seriously hurt.

"Baylee!" Lila called frantically down the hall, then stood stock still and listened for a response. A soft shuffling noise perked her ears. With Chloe on her heels, Lila followed the sounds, pressing her ear to several doors before coming to a stop outside one roughened by time to a silvered gray. A muffled cry resounded as Lila and Chloe threw it open to find Baylee in a heap on the ground.

Chloe rushed to her side, crouching to release the gag that rendered Baylee unable to assure them she hadn't been harmed.

"Did he hurt you?" Lila asked, searching Baylee's eyes for clues.

"Not really, but my arms and hands are numb." She managed to whisper, as Lila tried to loosen the knotted rope binding her to the exposed support beam. Hands trembling, Lila let loose a slew of curse words when pulling and tugging only caused the rope to tighten.

"Miss Lila, step aside." Both women spun around at the sound of Antoine's lilting voice. "Let me help. I've got a pocket knife." After carefully cutting her free, he snapped a few photos with his camera phone, assured them he would make a full report and cooperate in any way necessary, then stepped into the hallway to keep watch.

"Javier!" Baylee's choked cry resounded as he burst through the door. Flanked by Lila and Chloe and wrapped in the throw Antoine had had the presence of mind to pull from the back of the sofa near his desk, she stared back at him. Dark circles under her eyes and slightly hollowed cheeks spoke eloquently of exhaustion, but when he suggested rest and a visit from the doctor, she adamantly refused.

"Did you get him? Is that how you found me?"

"The others are taking care of that now." Javier ran gentle hands over her to test for broken bones and to reassure himself she was okay.

"Take me to them. I've got information they'll need."

"Are you sure you're all right?"

Baylee raised her chin defiantly. "He didn't hurt

me, if that's what you mean. I'm fine, but now I'm seeing red. Let's end this."

He noticed she retained the blanket slung over her shoulders, though.

"Baylee's safe," Javier keyed up the radio's microphone and spoke in clipped tones, alerting Nate and Dalton to the developing situation. "We're bringing her down now. Is it clear? I don't want her seeing him right now." His first concern, at this point, was Baylee's safety. Getting Remy was still a priority, but not as high as making sure his family was out of harm's way.

"I'm not scared of him, Javi. I want to help." When he hesitated, she said, "Please, Javi. I need to do this for Tomas." She staggered to her feet, stiff from the position she'd been forced into for so many hours. The blanket slipped enough for him to see the raw, red marks where Remy had bound her wrists. The man would pay for that alone, Javier vowed.

"You will not confront Remy Vincent but I'll take you to Nate if he says he can keep that from happening." Baylee opened her mouth to protest, but Javier wouldn't hear of it and refused to continue the conversation until Nate issued the all clear.

Back in the suite, Nate quickly checked Baylee for

signs of shock or injury. Part of his focus remained on EV and Remy, while the others hovered around the recent captive. Soon, Baylee was firmly settled into a comfortably soft chair with a plate of food in her lap and a glass of water on the table at her elbow.

When he judged her color had returned enough to satisfy him, Javier said, "Okay, tell us what happened. Did you find any evidence?."

Baylee's eyes widened. "You mean you didn't find it? And he didn't..." Baylee searched their faces for the answer and saw only puzzlement. "Well, everything was going according to plan—I managed to snap several photos of some pretty damning evidence—until I left the room and came face to face with Remy himself. He chased me, dragged me to that empty room, and took my camera." A smile lit Baylee's face, and she continued, her voice full of derision toward Remy and smugness at what happened next.

"Didn't do him any good, though. I managed to pull the memory card and hide it before he caught me. Once he realized I had already stashed the evidence, he started making threats. I could tell he didn't have the stones to actually hurt me, so I kept my mouth shut as long as I could. I knew his texts from my phone wouldn't fool you for long, Javi."

Admiration shone in her eyes, and was reflected back in kind. Javier had underestimated the amount of sheer badassery his sister-in-law possessed; he wouldn't make that mistake again.

"Just one question. Where is the memory card now?"

"It should be in Chloe's closet. I shoved it in her bag of dry cleaning before he caught up to me. I'd have gotten away completely but I made a wrong turn and hit a dead end. When he threatened to ruin Garritek, I told him where it was, but if he didn't find it, the staff must have already gone through and collected the bags to take to the cleaners. I'm hoping they found the memory card and put it back in her jacket pocket."

Chloe's eyes widened in understanding. "That's what he was looking for in my room; that's why he used EV's key card to break in. He probably lifted it off her. It's not like EV to lose things." She muttered a few choice words describing Remy under her breath, and at a nod from Nate, disappeared through the connecting door.

In a few moments, she was back, eyes alight above a fierce grin, holding the SIM card aloft like a trophy. "What are we waiting for? Let's go see if we have enough to make sure he stays behind bars for the rest of his life." With a grin, she reached across him to slide the hard-won SIM card into the built-in reader of Javier's computer, which was still playing security footage.

As her slideshow popped up, Nate let out a low whistle. No wonder Remy had upped the ante and resorted to kidnapping; what scrolled across the screen amounted to several counts of identity theft, and a whole lot more. Baylee had hit pay dirt.

Chapter 19

Baylee and Javier weren't the only ones on the edge of their seats. This meant just as much for them as it did for Ponderosa Pines, and neither was going to let the opportunity to expose Remy Vincent slip by over something as trivial as an abduction. There would be time to process the experience once the job was complete.

"I'm going in." Her shoulders squared, EV sailed into the café several minutes after Remy had taken a seat. He watched her walk toward him, seeing only what he wanted to see. A fashionably late woman with a gleam in her eye that showed how much she wanted him. A foolish woman that he could have on a whim, and ultimately bend to his will. As usual, his ego cast a veil of fantasy over his judgment.

The skin on EV's hands crawled when he grasped them and kissed her on the cheek. He'd aimed for her lips but a last-second twist of her head foiled him.

She'd play her part, but some things went beyond the pale.

Over Remy's left shoulder, Dalton tossed her a thumbs up and an air kiss to make her smile. The simple gestures of support lifted some of the tension; she returned them with a wink that Remy assumed was for him.

Since half of her mission was to stall Remy while the search for Baylee continued, she indulged in small talk, lulling him into complacency by allowing him to order for her, and letting him hold her hand across the table. To keep him seeing her initial reaction to his touch, she avoided meeting his intense gaze with her own until her emotions were under control. The ruse worked in her favor, feeding his ego by allowing him to think his touch affected her deeply enough to bring out the blushing schoolgirl inside. The more relaxed he became, the more her senses sharpened.

Nate's voice whispered through the com, "Javi checked in, they've narrowed the search area, heading there now". It took extra attention not to react to the hope flaring through her.

Remy glanced around the room, "It's so crowded in here. Why don't I call the waitress back and have her send the food up to your room where we can be alone." His voice dropped to a suggestive timbre that had no effect on EV at all.

Too easy. Better make him work for it.

"I'm not sure I'm ready to take it to the next step. There's Dalton and—"

"Remember how good we were together? You can't tell me you've had anyone else who knows what you like the way I do. I want you, EV, and I think you want me."

A hollow sentiment coming from lying lips, but no matter, because EV was long past caring. The only thought in her mind now was to play him like a virtuoso.

"I do, but not yet. Chloe and Lila are having final dress fittings. They'll be done in a little while, and then they have plans for a full spa treatment. We'll have hours alone once they're gone. We could get dessert to go."

Why not? Remy thought, might as well take if it she's offering, "All I need is you and a bowl of chocolate sauce."

"Maybe we could give that one a go." Dalton spoke in her ear.

"Mmmm," EV's hum of agreement was meant for Dalton.

"I'm still here," Nate managed to convey embarrassment and disgust in one short statement.

Okay, you weasel. Let's see if we can pin down your motive. Is it me?

"Did you hate me so much?" EV assessed his emotions by watching his face closely. "Your folks missed you a great deal." A tinge or red color stained his neck when his throat tightened and his teeth clenched. She'd hit a nerve there, though he managed to quickly force any signs of it from his features.

Seemingly relaxed again, he said, "I've never hated you." Then he made the most honest statement she'd heard from him since he'd arrived, "Walking away without knowing it was my last chance to say goodbye to my folks is my biggest regret in life. If I'd known how things would turn out, I would have done things differently."

When she squeezed his hand this time, it was with some small amount of genuine feeling. "Their loss devastated the entire community; I can only imagine how your grandparents must have felt."

"I doubt that. Losing his son turned my grandfather into someone else." Face hardened, Remy practically bit off the words. "You have no idea what it did to his mind. It changed him completely."

Really? I'd have no idea?

EV forced herself not to let go of his hand when all she wanted to do was slap him with it.

"I think I might know a little about how that feels. I miss him every day." EV let her lashes veil her eyes while she watched his reaction to the mention of their child. It took him a few seconds to go there, and when he did, a chuffed out breath and an eyeroll presented eloquent evidence that he cared nothing for his lost son, but was annoyed with her for bringing it up in connection with the death of his parents.

"Let it go, EV. I'm not going to get into a discussion of the miscarriage with you. Now or ever." The veneer of charm peeled back to show the cheap, shallow base below his surface. Under the table, the hand that wasn't clasped in his clenched to drive nails into palm with brutal force. EV dropped her eyes before he saw the raw fury she struggled to control. In her ear, Dalton whispered soothing words of encouragement that helped her pull it together, as did the smiling face of the waitress who served her lunch.

As though nothing of note had passed between them, Remy changed the subject to the one he most preferred discussing: himself.

Well, that takes revenge against me for losing the baby off the table.

While he prattled on, EV ran through her mental list of possible motives. Most crimes were committed over love or money. Whether he was even capable of the first, she had no idea, so she decided to move on to the second. Nate's research hadn't turned up a solid connection between Remy and Gilmore. Remy's net worth far exceeded the assets of Gilmore and Ponderosa Pines combined. Yet, the line had to be tugged. The trouble was, she had no idea where to begin pulling at those particular threads. Stalling for time, she picked at her meal.

"I'm sorry; I'm talking your ear off." The candy coating was back on him; too bad EV knew the chewy center was made of something that looked similar to a Tootsie Roll, but was definitely not flavored with chocolate. "Can I confess something to you, EV?"

Nope. Nope. Nope.

"Of course," EV forced a smile that could have passed for genuine to anyone who didn't know her well; Remy included.

"I'm as nervous around you as a teenager trying to get to first base. The new hair, the new clothes--"

That happened before you even got here. EV's blood ran cold. *You've been watching me. For how long?*

"Seeing you here like this, touching you, knowing we're going to ..." his thumb brushed over the back of her hand. He mistook her shiver of disgust for interest, "I think I'm falling for you all over again."

Dalton muttered several uncomplimentary things about Remy into EV's ear before Nate's voice commanded silence. Her delighted smile at hearing them worked in her favor when Remy took it to mean she felt the same.

Now what? She thought.

As though answering her mental question, Nate instructed, "Humor him."

"This is all very flattering, but we lead such different lives."

"It doesn't have to be that way, you could come with me. You know things were better when we were alone together," scorn made his next words sound like an epithet, "away from that...hole of a town."

And there it was again, the contempt he always shown for Ponderosa Pines. Could it be that it was the entire town he hated, and not any one member specifically? The town wouldn't fold without her, if that's what he thought. Was it?

Might as well ask. "Why do you hate Ponderosa Pines so much?"

"That place killed my parents."

"It was an accident, it could have happened at any time. How is that the town's fault?

"If they hadn't been heading off to try and convert more people to backwoods living, they would still be alive and my grandmother wouldn't have..." He swallowed twice. Hard.

Her ear piece erupted, "They've found Baylee— safe and sound and on her way back here. The locals will be here soon, and we need him out of the way before that happens. It's time to move this operation upstairs," Nate's message was a welcome one; both because Baylee was safe, and that it meant this whole ordeal was coming to a close. Dalton, dropping into a stooped, limping gait, circled toward the exit with his face averted. He meant to be in place before Remy put a single foot in EV's suite.

"Wouldn't have what? Tell me what happened." EV pulled her attention back from the external goings-on and seized on Remy's unfinished sentence. He'd let something important slip.

"Remy's grandmother passed peacefully in her sleep according to what I can find online." Nate caught on quickly that they'd finally hit on something. Busy fingers flew over his keyboard, and as they appeared, he whispered his findings into her ear. "I'll pull up the coroner's report, see if there's more to the story. Either way, you've hit a nerve, poke it harder."

"It killed her."

Sympathy painted EV's eyes with compassion while her mind spun like a top. Several possible outcomes played through her mind, each one giving him motive for revenge. This was it, maybe not the whole story, but the beginning of it, anyway. A wild elation bubbled up inside her.

She tamped it down, thinking hard on how to draw the rest from him.

"I only met her that one time, but your grand-mother seemed like a lovely person. I'm sorry for you, and for your grandfather."

A muscle twitched at the side of Remy's mouth, signaling a rush of negative emotion. To EV, it looked like annoyance, which seemed an odd reaction given the conversation. Her head tilted left while she let him see her assessing his state of mind. Now was not the time to hammer at him, she decided; instead, she needed to force impatience back and become his confidant.

"Would you feel better if you talked about it? Not here, though, up in my room."

Anticipation flared in his eyes. "Lead the way."

The minute the door closed, he turned to and bracketed her against it, leaning in to capture her lips with his. She just managed to slip her hand between his mouth and hers. "No, Remy. I want all the ghosts cleared from between us before we take that next step. Please, tell me about your grandmother, what happened to her?"

For a full minute or more, he stayed silent, his posture slowly changing while she thought he battled the decision to tell her some part of the truth, all of it, or to continue with the facade he had built. When another pang of sympathy surfaced, EV gave in to it and trusted her instincts. "I can see you're hurting," she gentled her voice, surprised to note the modicum of truth in her own words. She waited on the edge of what felt like all or nothing.

His arms dropped to his sides ending in tightly clenched fists. EV took the opportunity to move into the seating area. Reluctantly, he followed to settle beside her.

At his first words, she knew she'd won. "My grandmother went away after my father died. Not physically, just somewhere inside herself where no one could touch her. It was like something inside her had gone with him to wherever it is people go when they pass, and nothing we did could make her live again." His eyes, when they met hers, held the kind of pain that can suck a man under. Some small part of her felt sorry for him. "Grandfather couldn't reach her, and when I couldn't either, he blamed me for her falling into that state to begin with." He swallowed hard, and she watched the pain slide back down to his gut where it fed the fiery rage always simmering there.

Okay, then what colossal leap of intellect did you take that landed an entire town on your revenge list? Blurting out her inner dialog wasn't one of EV's problems; her internal filters were, if anything, too strict most of the time.

"That must have made you feel awful."

Red crept back up to color his face, "My parents walked away from everything to 'give their child a chance to connect to the earth'," he singsonged mockingly. "It was my fault they were there in the first place, and Grandfather made it clear that it was my duty—my family legacy—to make it right in the end."

"Make it right how?"

"Sometimes the law turns a blind eye," he spit out. "Some things you just have to do for yourself."

"We'll see about that," Dalton's voice hummed over the radio.

"What did you do, Remy?" An edge crept into her tone that, in his zeal, he failed to notice. "How can I be with you if you're going to keep secrets from me?"

He wanted to tell her; the need to lay his sins out in a row before her was almost stronger than the ego-swollen thirst to finish what he had started.

The moment spun out in deafening silence. He wasn't going to go through with it, she knew when the battle inside him finally ended when the smarmy look indicating he was about to move on her again came over his face.

"It's nothing. I swear. Didn't we come up here to have some fun?"

In her ear, Nate whispered the words she'd been waiting to hear, "Baylee's evidence was in Chloe's closet. We think he'll try to retrieve it. You should let him."

She let him think his distraction worked. "I need to freshen up first. I won't be a minute." EV made a beeline for the bathroom. The second she was gone, Remy launched off the sofa and silently pulled open Chloe's bedroom door. The dry cleaning, shrouded in plastic, hung in plain sight. EV heard the rustling of the bag through the cracked open bathroom door; hurriedly closed it again when she heard him coming back. He was back in his place, a smug smile on his face when she entered the room.

He rose to meet her halfway, his intention plainly to lead her to her bed.

A split second decision lay before EV, and a wrong choice now could lead to disaster. Should she keep stroking his ego by making him think she would follow him anywhere, no matter what laws he had broken? Or should she go for the proverbial knee to the nuts and play on his extreme dislike of being bested at anything?

"You know what? It's okay, you don't need to tell me." Feigned interest fell off her face to be replaced by a hard, speculative stare. She leaned back in her chair nonchalantly. "I already know most of it, anyway."

An eyebrow shot up before he could catch himself. Quickly, he forced it back down while relaxing his facial muscles into a less shocked arrangement. No way she knew. No way. "What are you talking about? You always did have a vivid imagination. There's nothing to tell. Why don't we go back to my room and talk about us?"

"I don't think so, Remy. Just out of curiosity, what did you have on Evan Plunkett."

The name dropped like a boulder to land between them, and Remy flinched.

"That's really the only thing I can't get a handle on about your whole scheme. How did he figure into it all?"

"I don't know any Evan Plunkett."

"Oh, I think you do. You blackmailed him." Remy cut his eyes toward the door—a sure sign he was thinking of bolting. He wouldn't get far in any case, but she preferred to skewer him right here and now. "What on earth made you choose him of all people? A braggart—" she sent up a little apology for speaking ill of the dead, "—with a limited sphere of influence.

You truly do have a poor sense of judgment when it comes to choosing evil minions." EV pursed her lips and slowly shook her head.

Without giving him time to reply, she needled him again."You actually did Ponderosa Pines a favor. While we're not going to be annexed by Gilmore any time soon—ever, really—working closely with the leaders over there paved the way for a reconciliation of sorts. A new respect on both sides, if you will."

His temper was fast on the way into red-line territory.

"You're crazy, you know that? I offer you everything you could ever want, and you come at me with some trumped up conspiracy theory." He curled his lip, but his sarcasm fell flat.

"I'm sorry, you're probably right. Frankly, I don't think you're smart enough to go to such elaborate lengths." She smiled brightly and pushed him over the brink. "But I do think you're petty enough to ruin someone else's life just to make yourself feel better. Or wait, maybe you were just your grandfather's little puppet. Did it hurt when he pulled your strings?"

"You bitch," he leaned toward her, venom practically dripping from his tongue. "You have no idea what I'm capable of." His hand closed over her arm with a painfully tight grip.

Here it comes, just like in books and movies, the stupid criminal monologue.

"Grandfather knew, though. He trusted me to make it right. To rip that town apart the same way my family was torn apart. Everything I tried failed, until I met Evan Plunkett at a hotel in Atlantic City. He was supposed to be in Boston attending an investing seminar. Instead, he was drunk, and into the house for more money than he made in a year."

None of that surprised EV, or anyone else from Ponderosa Pines listening to the conversation.

"When he started bawling about how he could get the money if they'd just let him go back to Ponderosa Pines for it. He swore he was a big shot with access to town funds, and I knew this was my one chance to have someone on the inside. I paid his tab, took him back to his room, sobered him up, and let him tell me all about his little town."

Tiny droplets of saliva splashed over her face, his was so close. She did not flinch.

"It took me a month or so to put together a good enough cover to keep him from figuring out who I was, and then I played the angles. Let him loose on your beloved elders while I posed as someone else and established contact with an elected official in Gilmore."

EV let all the scorn she could muster infuse her voice, "Worked out real well for you, didn't it? Ponderosa Pines is intact, stronger than ever. Your cover wasn't so solid, either. Tomas Delarosa is Javier's half brother."

His eyebrows shot toward his hairline.

"Looks like you didn't do your homework, Remy. And now, you're busted."

"Hell I am," the hand not clutching her arm reached into his pocket to pull out a SIM card. "I've already destroyed the documents and now, here's your evidence." The card hit the floor and Remy ground it to pieces under his heel. "You'll never prove a thing."

Dark vengeance painted itself across her face as she wrenched her arm free. Turning, she pulled up her shirt so he could see the wire. "Really? I think I will."

Furious at being beaten by the one woman he was sure he could control, Remy did exactly what Dalton had sworn he would never allow; lifted arm and backhanded EV with all his strength. Where his hand landed, her cheek stung and burned; a bruise already forming. He only had a second to lean over her, sneering, before Dalton flew from EV's bedroom where he had been watching.

"What did I tell you?" Dalton grabbed Remy's shoulder and spun him around to face the consequences; Dalton's meaty fists being consequence one and consequence two. At this point, EV faced another hard choice. Remy had taken her by surprise, or he would never have landed the blow; now the desire to get up and practice her kickboxing skills on him was about as strong as any she'd ever known. But, there stood Dalton; fists raised, fight face on, and ready to defend her honor. With an internal grin, she decided to let him.

Remy had just enough time to open his mouth, but not enough to get out whatever taunt trembled on the tip of his tongue before Dalton landed a solid right punch, and EV had to scramble out of the way to avoid Remy's falling body. When Dalton reached down to help her up, Nate burst through the connecting door with two members of the Garda right behind.

The white cat stalked out the door of EV's bedroom where he had hidden yet again, took one look at Remy, and hissed. The sound brought a smirk to EV's face.

Leaving Remy to their less-than-tender mercies, Dalton slung an arm around EV's waist, and guided her into Lila's suite without a backward glance.

Chapter 20

With Remy locked up and Baylee safe, Chloe and EV decided to take a page from Lila's book and put together a fabulous bachelorette party. When they checked with Antoine to see if he could help with preparations, his response overwhelmed. Chloe gave him a few ideas that would put Lila where she was happiest —in the spotlight. Within minutes, he had marshaled his forces and had a group of staff minions ready to do his bidding.

Spurred by a series of increasingly insistent calls from Lila, Chloe was forced to leave everything in Antoine and EV's capable hands, and go join her mother and Javier in greeting new arrivals.

Wedding guests and participants had begun trickling in early that morning, which meant the guest list for the bachelorette party grew by the hour. Cousin Faith and her husband arrived right on time;

closely followed by several carloads of Javier's family, flown in first-class from their home near Madrid.

"Chloe, this is Javier's mother, Concetta; his sisters, Della and Karmen, and their husbands, Luis and Sal; and cousins Victor, Iliana, and Edita." Lila pointed at each in turn, then, noticing the look on Chloe's face whispered, "You don't have to remember them all right now; don't worry."

After being showered with more cheek kisses than she could count, and having been squeezed practically to death by a bevy of delighted, soft-skinned Spaniards, Chloe began to understand how easily Lila had been drawn into Javier's close-knit family. They made her feel included, even loved, within minutes of meeting them.

Baylee barely made it down the stone steps toward the milling horde before being surrounded and eventually shuffled out of sight. Tomas was hoping to be cleared to travel the next day, but Chloe was sure Baylee was in good hands until then. Earlier in the day, Antoine had delivered the welcome news that no charges would be filed against Baylee or Javier for breaking into Remy's room, provided they both testify when his case came to court. In trade, Remy would plead out to a lesser offense on the kidnapping charges. He'd still be spending most of his twilight years in a correctional facility, but it would be a minimum security one versus a federal penitentiary.

And then, Lila dropped a bombshell on Chloe. "You'll be meeting your new step siblings later on today," she said, as though this wasn't entirely new information.

"My new what?" Chloe couldn't process the words. "You couldn't have told me before?"

"You didn't ask," A trace of rebuke was softened by a smile. "We were busy and things have been frantic. It never came up."

A dozen thoughts crowded into Chloe's mind. How many siblings was she about to gain? Would they like her? Being an only child had its privileges, and yet it had also, at times, meant for a lonely childhood. Changing schools, leaving friends behind, and never having anyone else with the same experiences had left more of a hole in Chloe than she realized. It might be late in the game, but sisters and brothers, if they were anything like the rest of the clan she'd met so far, weren't an entirely horrible prospect. Nerve wracking maybe, but good.

"How many siblings am I about to get? Are they

younger or older?" The questions came rapid fire. "Do they know about me, at least?"

Lila held up a hand to stop Chloe talking, "Three. A sister and two brothers. All younger, but not by a lot. They can't wait to meet you."

"You still could have told me."

"Yes, Dear, but it wouldn't have been nearly as much fun."

The sun hung low on the horizon when Javier's progeny made their arrival. In style—in a helicopter with the Garritek logo emblazoned across the side. The whirlybird touched down just long enough to discharge it's passengers, then lifted off quickly. As it rose into the sky, Chloe felt like it took her stomach along with it.

Javier rushed ahead to greet them while Lila and Chloe hung back, allowing them a moment. She experienced a moment of envy when Javier greeted his daughter by picking her up and giving her a whirl as though she were eight years old instead of closer to twenty-eight. It was a father/daughter thing, she supposed. Not that she'd had any experience with those. Chestnut curls framed a delicate face and played off the woman's full, red lips. Javier certainly made attractive children.

All the feelings of not fitting in roared back through Chloe like stampeding stallions when the young people greeted Lila with hugs and familiarity. Inch by inch, her spine stiffened, the old shields built up and up. She felt like a mile of distance separated her from them, and this time, it was worse, because her mother was on the other side of the divide, still talking animatedly with the sloe-eyed beauty.

"Chloe." Javier's questioning tone pulled Chloe back to focus. Flanking him, his two sons looked enough alike to be twins—twins who bore a marked resemblance to their father. The same white smiles, smooth olive skin, and warm, generous eyes. Only their hairstyles and clothing choices differed.

Fatherly pride radiated from Javier as he introduced first Cisco, who wore ripped jeans and a band tee—a shock of raven hair angled over his forehead, and then Miguel who favored his father's relaxed, yet classic style. Chloe wasn't sure what kind of greeting they expected, so she slapped on a tentative smile and held out her hand.

Before she had time to utter the first word of greeting, Chloe was nearly knocked over by five feet-two inches of dynamite. "I am Bianca. I have wanted so long to have a sister and all I get are these two—" Bianca let go of Chloe and waved a dramatic arm toward her two brothers. "Come, we will go inside, get a nice limoncello and get to know one another." It wasn't like she had a choice; Bianca possessed a firm grip and an iron determination. Her smile, though, was warm, and thawed Chloe's resistance. She let the chattering Bianca lead her away with only a short backward glance, which showed Lila looking slightly misty.

When Lila had described Javier's mother, Concetta, as a firecracker, she couldn't have been more on point. Shorter than Chloe by almost a foot, and nearly as round as she was tall, Concetta possessed a certain *joie de vivre*, even at her advanced age. Cha-cha-cha-ing across the pub stage, singing a spirited karaoke version of an old disco-era tune in beautiful Spanish, she had everyone in the audience on their feet. With a final bow and a conspiratorial wink in Chloe's direction, she handed off the microphone to Lila once more.

In another life, Chloe's mother might have had a very successful singing career, and Lila never turned down an opportunity to display her talented pipes. As she took the stage for at least the tenth time that night with naked glee, Chloe knew they had hit the bachelorette party nail on the head.

No inappropriate phallic-shaped ice cubes or embarrassing plastic tiaras for Lila; two-hundred-dollar bottles of Crystal flowed like water into Swarovski flutes alongside caviar-covered toast points and pate de foie gras. Maybe the karaoke wasn't in keeping with the otherwise five-star accommodations, but the juxtaposition was wholly *Lila*.

Over the evening, instead of dwindling, the crowd swelled for a time as more new arrivals stopped in for a bit of the bubbly, and few minutes of hobnobbing with the bride-to-be. She sang a few more songs, and even dragged Chloe and up on stage to harmonize while EV got into a long discussion on the merits of hugelkultur gardening beds with one of Javi's sisters, also an avid vegetable grower.

Hours later, when the party finally wound down, Lila, EV, Chloe, and Javier's family settled around a large round table in the quieter section of the room. Talk turned to anecdotes and marriage advice—mostly given by the women in Javier's family, since Faith was the only married member of the wedding party. Lila listened politely to cautions of how love changes over time with the intention of ignoring every word completely. It had taken her this long to find Javier and whatever the future might bring, one thing was certain, they would handle it together.

"I was afraid my Javi would never find love again," Concetta's brown eyes twinkled merrily, if a little tipsily, "you make him happy. My blessing upon you both."

Hoping for a good night message from Nate, Chloe pulled her phone out of a purse so dainty, it hardly had room for anything else. The first thing she saw was an email notification from Wesley:

Hey Chlo,

Just following up with that info you wanted. I stumbled onto a site with cached archives of a few gossip rags, and finally found some usable information.

What followed after was an illuminating series of snippets that quickly came together to paint an unflattering picture.

Bingo. Oh, Hannah, you've been a naughty girl.

It seemed Ms. Frank had been either hard up for some extra cash, or so intent on building her business that she forgot to protect her clients' privacy. As an insider, she had access to a plethora of private details surrounding several five-star celebrity weddings, and hadn't hesitated to sell their secrets—and a few photographs—to any print or online magazine willing to pay big bucks.

Though not technically illegal, the breech in trust prompted a few high-profile clients to spread the word. It looked like an attempt at damage control had pulled the mentions from the sites, but not from the independent archives. Even then, it hadn't been enough, and Hannah's business tanked. Lila was right; this was her last chance at salvaging her career, and Chloe guessed she would stop at nothing to get back into Tinseltown's good graces.

"I think it's time we headed off to bed. Good thing we've got a day between now and the wedding, because I doubt any of us are going to be at our best in the morning." EV squinted at her watch. It was past 2:00 am and she'd gone beyond her typical number of alcohol servings. She wasn't drunk, but she wasn't sober, either. The pub was nearly empty since the Rosales clan had succumbed to too many glasses of champagne and trickled off to bed. Only the bride, Chloe, Faith, and Baylee remained. A chorus of agreement resounded.

Lila stifled a yawn and surveyed the room, her eyes narrowing as something—or someone—caught her attention. "In a minute; there's something we've got to take care of."

"Not so fast, Hannah Banana. Hand it over." Chloe breathed down Hannah's neck, as Lila, EV, Faith and Baylee surrounded the woman, who searched for an escape, but to no avail. "We saw you snapping photos with your little camera phone; and I've been monitoring your Twitter and Facebook feeds. We know you've been stalking us, pretending to be Lila's right hand; and we know you've contacted *The Tattler* offering pics of my mother's wedding in exchange for cash. I've got my connections, same as you."

"I don't know what you're talking about. I was just grabbing a quick drink, and now I think I'll head up to my room." EV, Faith, and Baylee linked arms, positioning themselves between Lila and Chloe, and forcing Hannah to remain seated.

"How dare you try and capitalize on my wedding!" Lila nearly shrieked. Chloe almost felt sorry for Hannah, considering the verbal assault she was about to endure—almost, but not quite. "I told you no when you called me a month ago; told you I was perfectly capable of planning my own wedding. You must realize I have friends and acquaintances all over the globe, so I know you know that I'm well aware you pulled a few shenanigans. Using low-quality products and charging premium prices! That's just sad!"

This was a new one for Chloe, but it didn't come as much of a shock, given Hannah's other indiscretions. "You're lucky you got off on a technicality," Chloe interjected, "and weren't sent to jail for breech of privacy when you started selling photos to the gossip rags. But your little game is up; get a life, and get a real job!"

Lila snatched the phone away from Hannah and began to scroll through the photo gallery. Disgust etched further into her face with each swipe, until finally she plunked the device into Hannah's own half-empty drink. "Try getting anything useful off that, now!" She spat. "And if I ever—I repeat, ever—see an unauthorized photograph of me, my family, or my wedding that even so much as carries your sickly-sweet scent, I'll bankrupt you in legal fees so fast your little bobble-head will spin. Do I make myself clear?"

Hannah's shoulders shook with silent sobs, left her phone and drink at the bar and scuttled out of the room without another word. The second she disappeared around the corner, grins spread across the five women's faces as they gazed at each other in turn.

A low whistle escaped EV's lips. "Remind me never to get on either of your bad sides!"

"I'll drink to that!" Faith ordered a round of fruity pink shots before dragging them all onto the dance floor for one last song, late hour be damned.

Chapter 21

Now that the moment of truth was upon her, EV wouldn't let a little thing like a mild hangover and a black eye stop her from seeing Dalton. Dealing with Remy's arrest had taken up half the night after they'd gotten a confession out of him. The next morning, he'd been incredibly patient when wedding duties kept her from finding a quiet moment to spend with him. The best she'd been able to do was exchange a shrug and a smile each time she'd caught sight of him. He'd checked on her throughout the day, and each glimpse of him watching over her sent her heart racing, pooled heat in her belly. With the bachelorette party behind them, and the wedding tomorrow, Lila had scheduled today as time to spend with Javier's family, leaving EV completely free.

When they came together this time, no ghosts would stand between them.

Chloe's note on the bedside table read:

Faith fell asleep in my bed, so Nate and I are taking hers, which leaves Dalton all alone. Don't tell Mother where I am until at least noon, and don't be an idiot. Go to him.

Impertinent brat.

Yet, the wisdom was undeniable, and EV meant to do just that. She brushed the morning-after fuzziness from her teeth, downed a glass of water, and let the hot spray from the shower beat away the last of the cobwebs. A headline on one of those women-shouldn't-take-crap-from-anyone-but-they-should-still-look-good magazines in the gift shop insisted that Fifty is the New Thirty. A frank assessment of her body in the mirror told her she still looked good, but maybe not thirty-good. So what if her butt was moving south for the winter, and her breasts rode a little closer to her waist. She wasn't too old for a new love, right? If there was anything in her life to regret, it was having spent way too much time hoarding her secret pain like a broody hen.

Having her loss dragged kicking and screaming out into the light had tamed it from a hideous monster to a healing wound she could carry without bending under the weight. Telling someone—being vulnerable enough to share the burden—takes strength, but not as much as it does to carry alone. Ridiculous to be learning something so basic, so seemingly simple a lesson at her age.

Even now, two days later, the truth of why Remy had turned to revenge left her feeling like she imagined Dorothy felt when she first laid eyes on the humbug masquerading as the great and powerful Oz. A deathbed promise to an old man with dementia was a flimsy excuse for the actions that had turned Tomas into collateral damage.

All of that was over now, and, grateful for the distraction, EV realized her feet had carried her to Dalton's door. She swallowed the irrational fear that he might have changed his mind, and tapped rapidly but lightly to find out; her heart rapped to the same beat in her chest.

Then the door opened, and she was in his arms, and he was kissing her. Deep, drugging kisses that sent tingling heat all the way down to her toes. She pressed against him, whispered over his lips, "mine," and "more."

Before he tumbled her to the bed, Dalton answered with a single word, "Forever."

Later, Dalton leaned up on one elbow to look

down at her. "How are you feeling?" He lifted a broad hand to brush a lock of hair from her face, scowling at the mark where Remy had hit her. "You should see the other guy," she joked. Dalton didn't see the humor. "It doesn't hurt, honest."

"I failed, and he got his hands on you."

"Not where it counts. He touched my face, but you touched my soul."

His gaze turned solemn. EV turned her face until he cupped the tender flesh with his hand. "I love you," She said the words he needed to hear, because if she didn't, she was afraid they might burn their way out of her.

Everything he felt for her was there in his eyes. Hers fluttered closed, then opened to show him all the shadows had gone. A quiet knock on the door leading from Lila's room to the castle hallway interrupted her nightly beauty ritual. After removing her makeup, applying a creamy, anti-aging mask, and a thick layer of night cream, she was finishing the routine with a roll-on eye serum. She needed to look her best tomorrow.

Though the drama seemed to have subsided, but since she'd banished Javier for the night so he couldn't possibly see her in her dress before the wedding, Lila looked through the peephole before opening the door, and was surprised to see Nate's face distorted by the curved lens.

"Is everything alright? Is it Chloe?"

"No, no. Everything is fine. I was hoping I could talk to you about something." Lila ushered him inside, indicating that he take a seat on the sofa while she perched next to him.

Nate did as directed, leaning over to place his elbows on his knees, nervous energy spilling out of every pore. She remained silent, waiting for the question she knew he was about to ask.

"I want you to know that I love your daughter more than anything in this world. I get the feeling you're not so thrilled about that, and I'd like to know why." This wasn't the path Lila expected; she was being put on the spot, and that wasn't something she was used to.

Lila sighed; she knew she had been less than hospitable toward Nate, and realized that he had shown nothing but care and concern for her Chloe. What more could a mother ask for? It might be time to let him off the hook.

"Chloe has been my whole world; she's everything to me. I've been lonely since she moved back to

Ponderosa Pines. At some point, I figured, she'd tire of provincial life and things would get back to normal." Lila stalled by brushing at an imperceptible bit of lint on her pants. "I thought I was giving her a life of adventure, the kind of life I dreamed of when I was her age. Instead, it turns out all she wanted was to settle down and stay in one place. Best laid plans, I suppose." The fidgeting hand moved to rest on his arm.

"I have nothing against you; in fact, I encouraged her to go after what she wanted. But, I had to make sure you weren't going to try to clip her wings. I can see that you want her to be happy, and that you'd go to the ends of the earth to ensure that she is."

Nate interjected gently but firmly, "You know this means you're going to have to butt out now, right? I can only handle so much interference."

"I will, I promise. And I'm sorry for making you feel like you had something to prove. You'll understand, someday, when you have children of your own," she punctuated the statement with a pointed look, "the overwhelming need to meddle. Can you forgive me?" Nate doubted many people had ever been on the receiving end of a Lila LaRue apology, and accepted it without further to-do.

"You realize I'm not going to bow out gracefully, and that means you and I will be spending time together. Hopefully, as family."

Lila's encouraging smile gave Nate permission to ask the big question. "I want to marry Chloe more than I've ever wanted anything in my entire life. Your blessing would mean a lot to me, and to her. Do I have your permission to propose?"

Tears sprung to Lila's eyes as she enveloped Nate in an unguarded hug. "Of course, you do. Take care of my baby."

"I will."

Chapter 22

Lila stood on a pedestal surrounded by mirrors, watching the admiring faces of her beloved bridal party. Baylee knelt before her, the clicking of her camera audible above the din of a hundred anxious guests waiting in the next room for Lila's entrance.

EV, sporting enough pancake makeup to cover her bruises, produced a small velvet box from the bag of emergency supplies Chloe insisted they put together "just in case".

"Lila, I have something for you, something *old.*" With a tender smile, she lifted the lid and removed a single, 24-karat gold, diamond-encrusted hairpin.

Lila gasped. "I can't believe you remembered this! You're going to make me cry and ruin my makeup!"

"My mother had a whole set of these; six in all." EV explained to Chloe and Faith. "We used to play with them as kids, can you imagine? There wasn't much use for this kind of trinket in Ponderosa Pines, so she sold them and used the money to help construct the turbines that now power the town. I think it was more about making a statement than actually needing the money. But she kept this one as a memento, and I thought…" EV's voice tightened, and when she looked up at Lila, her eyes were swimming with unshed tears.

"It's perfect, and I love you. Thank you." EV slid the pin into place and stepped back to appraise the bride. "It's also a loaner; I might need it one of these days." She added with a wink.

"So that's old and borrowed; your necklace is new; now we just need something blue." Chloe looked around the room in a panic. Of all the things to forget.

Lila lifted her dress, exposing one shapely leg and pointed to a lacy garter edged in blue satin. "All set. Let's get this show on the road."

The ceremony went off without a hitch; Lila practically sailed down the aisle, and vows were exchanged above sniffles from an emotional audience. Chloe, grateful for the wonder of waterproof mascara, shed tears of joy at the depth of love she saw on both Lila's and Javier's faces. As they said their vows, EV noticed the look passing between Chloe and Nate; deducing that it wouldn't be long before they made pronouncements of their own. By the time Mr. & Mrs. Javier Rosales made their entrance into the Rose Room, Chloe's eyes were dry and beaming.

All of Lila's careful planning had paid off: soft, twinkling lights sparkled off beveled crystal at every place setting; the pale blue bridesmaids dresses provided inspiration for a neutral gray, silver, and gold color scheme punctuated with sapphire accents; and a decadent blue velvet cake covered in fondant and white chocolate roses elicited a chorus of *oohs* and *ahhs* when cut.

A delayed flight had given Javier and Tomas mere moments to reconnect before they had to take their places at the front of the room. After Baylee's emotional phone call to tell Tomas of Remy Vincent's arrest and that all charges against Tomas had been dropped, his attorneys had moved heaven and earth to get his travel documents reissued so he could get to the castle in time for the wedding.

Watching his brother stride into the lobby, take his wife in his arms, and kiss the breath out of her released the last weight from Javier's heart. When

Tomas stood to deliver his best man speech, it was with more confidence and poise than he had displayed for quite some time.

"To my big brother—my hero—and his beautiful bride: thank you for the unending support you have provided me, even in my darkest hour. It's been a difficult year for me, and you've stuck by me through thick and thin. I can't tell you how much that means to me." His gaze broke from where it hovered between Javier and Lila, searching for Baylee, whose teary-eyed expression was full of hope for the first time in too long.

"Lila, I know you can take care of yourself; you're an exceptional woman. But from now on, you've got a partner who, I can attest, will never fail to support you and fight for you. We should all strive to be the husband I know Javi will be. Love you both!"

Everyone toasted, the newlyweds exchanged besotted kisses, and when Chloe saw a camera flash, she knew Baylee had captured the moment.

The party continued long into the night. Two hunky bartenders and a few kitchen staffers offered to stay and keep the food hot and the drinks flowing; Chloe noticed a tip jar full to bursting, even though Lila's tab included a generous gratuity. She guessed they'd serve until dawn, if given the opportunity. Noticing a break in the steady stream of well-wishers who had monopolized most of Lila and Javier's evening, Chloe gathered EV, Nate, and Dalton and whisked the happy couple into a changing room reserved for the bridal party.

"Something arrived in my email yesterday afternoon; a gift for you two. I forwarded you a copy, but I thought it would be appropriate if we all took a look at it now." Chloe explained while booting up her laptop. "Congratulations from Ponderosa Pines."

A few clicks opened a video, beginning with a panoramic view of Ponderosa Pines that Chloe could tell had been filmed from atop the church bell tower. Sparkling snow clung to every tree branch, covered every roof, and formed fluffy banks along each winding road through town. The village looked like a winter wonderland, and Chloe appreciated Javier's involuntary, awed gasp at the sight. "Congratulations, Lila & Javier!" scrawled across the screen in glitter script, as if written with the wave of a magic wand.

Swirling into a pinwheel, the scene changed to a view of the town square where, it seemed, the entire town had gathered. A chorus of congratulations broke out over the notes of Pachelbel's *Cannon*. Everyone waved and blew kisses at the camera, and when Chloe peeled her eyes from the screen there wasn't a dry eye among the group.

Priscilla Lewellyn's face appeared on the screen; she was sitting in the back room of Thread, surrounded by skeins of yarn and backdropped by an intricate quilt depicting an aerial map of Ponderosa Pines. "Hello, Lila and Javier. We all wanted you to know that we're so happy for you, and we wish you both a lifetime of happiness. You are in our thoughts, and we hope you'll make it home for a visit one of these days!" As Priscilla and Thread faded into the background, Lottie and Talia swirled into focus.

"Watch out, Javier, you married one spitfire of a woman!" Lottie warned, an uncharacteristically warm smile emblazoned across her face. Apparently, Lila was one of the few people on Lottie's good side —probably due to her significantly distant proximity. "And you must be one hell of a man if she chose to spend the rest of her life with you." The statement was punctuated by a suggestive wiggling of eyebrows and a sly smile that actually brought a blush to Javier's face.

Continuing on for several more minutes, a good

percentage of the town expressed their congratulations, some including a story or anecdote about Lila's youth, and all urging the couple to plan a visit to the Pines as soon as possible. When the last image faded from the screen, a teary-eyed Lila took turns embracing each of the five of them before returning to her place at Javier's side.

"Damn those crazy old bats!" Lila exclaimed, wiping her face with a dainty white handkerchief. "Now I'm going to have to visit." She shot a meaningful look at EV, knowing her friend would recall Lila's promise to return when EV married Dalton. EV rolled her eyes in response, but shot a look at Dalton that spoke volumes in Lila's educated opinion.

"Well, I, for one, can't wait." Javier had caught the Ponderosa Pines bug; Chloe guessed she'd be seeing a lot more of her mother in the future. The thought put a smile on her face, and as she wrapped one arm around Nate's waist and the other around EV's, she couldn't help feel like everything was finally falling into place.

C hloe padded over to the kitchen in search of coffee, clad in one of Nate's button-down shirts, her hair disheveled. Humming to herself, she filled the carafe with water and set the machine to brew. As she leaned over the sink, Nate watched her from beneath a pile of fur blankets stretched in front of a roaring, rustic stone fireplace. *How did I get so lucky?* He thought, as Chloe stretched on her tiptoes to get a better view of the rolling Irish hillside encompassing the cottage's backyard, and revealing her long, lean legs.

Nate watched her for a long moment, then stole to the entryway and pulled a small box from his coat pocket. He was back before she realized he had moved, and when she returned with two steaming cups of coffee and pulled a fuzzy throw around her shoulders, Chloe still hadn't noticed the beatific expression on his face.

"We only have two more days here." Chloe lamented. "I'm excited about going home, but I also don't want to leave. I like spending my days and nights with you. And I don't want you to go back to your father's house." She finished quietly, not quite meeting his gaze. She didn't want to push her luck; make him feel like she wanted more than he was ready to give. But if she was honest with herself, Chloe knew her feelings ran deep—and she hoped they were on the same page.

Nate pulled himself into a sitting position, set his cup on a nearby end table and leaned toward her. He gently placed a finger under her chin and lifted Chloe's face until they were looking into one another's eyes. "I don't want to go back either. I want to stay with you, forever. I love you, Chloe." As he spoke, Nate shifted onto his knees and pulled the box from where it was stashed between two pillows.

"I've always loved you, and I want to spend the rest of my life making you happy. Will you make me the happiest man alive?" And with that, he opened the box and held his breath as he watched her expression change from casual excitement to gleeful incredulity. Nestled inside the box was a ring that would make any woman sing; a vintage, white gold pave band sparkled in the firelight, twisting around an exquisite, princess-cut diamond at least two carats in weight.

It was beautiful, but Chloe would have said yes to whatever had come out of a Cracker Jack box. Her breath caught in her throat as she realized this wasn't a dream—she really would get to keep Nate by her side forever. Wrapping her arms around his neck with a vice-like grip, Chloe answered Nate's question with a deep, head-swimming kiss. When she finally released him, her jubilant "yes" left no room for doubt.

Thank you so much for reading! We know you're wondering what will happen next in Ponderosa Pines.

Keep reading for a preview of the next book, Bait and Snitch, where Chloe and EV not only solve a murder, but help two people find love!

Quick Author's Note

If you weren't already aware, ReGina and Erin are a mother/daughter writing team, and yes, that means we mix family and work - with all the ups and downs you might expect. It helps that we basically share a single brain most of the time and tend to finish each other's sentences...literally. It also means we sometimes squabble over plot points, but since we're best friends, too, we let that stuff roll right off our backs.

This is the first series we ever wrote together, and it holds a special place in our hearts. Fun fact! In the book, the town's name of Ponderosa Pines came about as a compromise between the couple who founded the town. In reality, it came from the name of the apartment building Erin was living in at the time!

We intended to set the story in a similar apartment complex but as things went along, we ended with something just a bit quirkier. Ponderosa Pines is a place we'd both like to live.

In case you're wondering how we split up the work when we write together, we come up with a plot and scene list and then call dibs on which ones we want to write. In this case, Erin called all of the Chloe scenes while ReGina handled EV. As always, we go over each other's work once the book is done.

Anyway, if you've come this far with us and not decided we're complete and total whackadoodles... and especially if you have, we're offering a chance to sign up for our newsletters— the best place to get new release updates, sales notifications, and other fun content.

You can sign up for ReGina's newsletter here and/or Erin's newsletter here. As a thank-you gift for hanging out with us, you'll also get a FREE novella that isn't available anywhere else. And of course, we promise not to SPAM your inbox!

Love, hugs, and happy reading,
ReGina & Erin

P.S. If you enjoyed this book, it would be great if you

could leave a review or recommendation on your favorite store, GoodReads, or BookBub.

Your reviews help indie authors sell more books!

Excerpt from Bait and Snitch

PONDEROSA PINES
MYSTERIES - BOOK THREE

"Psst, over here!" Chloe LaRue's hoarse whisper was barely audible over the din of clinking silverware and several other conversations going on inside the Mudbucket, but EV Torrence spotted her friend the instant she passed through the door. Considering Chloe was the only one in the room wearing a head scarf and dark-rimmed sunglasses, she was hard to miss.

"Why, hello, Miss Monroe, fancy meeting you here." EV teased as she settled into a brightly painted chair across from Chloe. The eye roll behind Chloe's sunglasses was nearly audible to EV—and she had expected no less. Chloe tossed her shoulder-length blond hair and scrunched her slightly upturned button nose in EV's direction.

"You keep it up and your face will get stuck like

that. You'll have to spend the rest of your life looking at the insides of your eyelids."

"Ha ha. You're hilarious." Chloe slid the glasses up on her head, thought better of a second eye roll, and trained her wide chocolate-colored eyes on EV's face with effort. Sable hair hung in layers around EV's high, flushed cheekbones, and framed bright, sparkling green eyes. It was easy to see why people never believed EV was in her '50's; she exemplified how clean eating and regular exercise could slow the ravages of age.

EV grinned. "It's all right, I felt like I had to sneak around to get here, too. I took a seriously roundabout route through the woods and the east field. The fairy garden is not a peaceful place when you're snow-shoeing through it. Killed two birds with one stone, though, and got in my workout for the day!"

Now that Nate Harper was shacking up at Chloe's house, and EV had claimed half of Dalton Burnsoll's dresser drawers, the two best friends' nightly wanderings through the backyard path between their houses had decreased to infrequent at best. Both men would have understood the need for them to make time for each other, but it was much more fun to meet up like this—away from prying eyes and ears.

Sure, the clandestine nature of their time together may have been noticed by other residents of Ponderosa Pines, but it wasn't something Chloe would be commenting on in her column, 'Babble & Spin'. Nobody in town—save for EV and, of course, Nate—knew the identity of the mystery author, and this was one of those times Chloe would stoop to use the anonymity to her advantage. Reporting on her own relationships always made Chloe uncomfortable, but sometimes there was no way around it; no mention of herself or her close friends would arouse suspicion in the long run.

A town like Ponderosa Pines—boasting just over 500 residents, many of whom were descendants of the original 60's commune from which the hamlet had risen—thrived on gossip of any kind. EV's unofficial position as matriarch allowed her access to a bevy of information, and caused a contingent of townspeople to wonder whether she was responsible for the installment of snark printed in *The Pine Cone* each week. Not that she didn't contribute; but passing tidbits to Chloe for follow-up was as big a part as she wanted to play.

"So how is Nate adjusting to life in your itty bitty house?" EV asked with interest. Before Chloe could answer, an ever-expanding Rhonda Erickson waddled over to their table and barked, uncharacteristically, "What'll it be?" at the back of EV's head.

Spinning around in her chair, EV surveyed the pregnant woman and immediately rose to offer her aching feet a break. "Sit, now." She commanded before marching around the curved counter to make her own mocha cappuccino.

"I'm sorry, EV. Didn't mean to bite your head off. This baby is going to be fifteen pounds if he keeps growing like this. David's out picking up some supplies to finish the nursery, and the last hour has felt like five, at least." She rolled her neck back and forth, pinching the bridge of her nose as if to stave off an oncoming headache.

"No problem, I still remember how to steam milk. Did I ever tell you I helped Dalton out a few times when he owned the place? Marlene felt about like you do right before she had Carrie, so I pulled a few shifts while they looked for someone to replace her."

"Well, thanks for giving me a minute to catch my breath. That mocha is on me; Chloe's too. I'm sure I'll see you ladies in here tomorrow for another private chat." A quick wink let EV know that Rhonda had noticed their seemingly-innocent increase in caffeine cravings, but wouldn't share their secret with anyone else.

"You call me when you have that baby; I'm volunteering to lend a hand. All it will cost you is a few baby cuddles." With no children of her own, EV's only chance at sniffing baby heads came vicariously. With Chloe and Nate all snugged up, she was hoping for a pink or blue bundle to come along soon. Auntie EV had a nice ring to it, and was the only tolerable option. Calling EV by her given name of Emmalina was a big no-no, and being referred to as Auntie Em was simply out of the question.

Rhonda smiled ruefully and patted her stomach. "If he ever decides to come out, I'll let you know."

"Do you have any family coming in for the happy event?" Rhonda wasn't one to talk about her family, which sparked Chloe's innate curiosity. "Both Inns are probably booked up by now, but I bet EV would be happy to bunk with Dalton and give up her place if a bed is needed." Chloe raised her voice so EV, who bustled around clearing tables and serving coffee, could hear her.

"Happy to." EV assured.

"Our folks all live up in the county—four, maybe five-hour drive depending on road conditions. Doc

Talbot says first babies always take a while, so we figured they'd all have time to get here once things start to roll. Mom says she's been going to bed fully dressed in case the call comes in the middle of the night." Rhonda grinned at the mental picture. "They'd have all been here and underfoot for the past week if I'd given the word. I'm already hormonal, I don't need a house full of well-meaning parents at the moment. But I think I'll take you up on that offer when the time comes if you're serious, EV."

"Just say the word." EV settled back in her seat. "So, Mata Hari, where's that seed catalog you promised to bring? Nothing like picking out flowers when it's threatening to snow."

Chloe plopped said catalog onto the table, fully a quarter of the page corners were turned down indicating they held items she was interested in planting. Alongside the catalog, she unfolded a sheet of graph paper with detailed outlines of what she planned for the year. By the time all her final choices had been penciled in, the threat of snow had become a reality.

· · ·

"A chocolate chip cookie? A chicken head? A needle threader?" EV shouted excitedly, a loud beeping noise cutting off the last guess.

"It was the Millennium Falcon!" Dalton cried over the sound of exuberant laughter filling Chloe's tiny living room. Curly dark hair with only a touch of gray at the temples framed eyes that grew laugh lines every time Dalton flashed the smile that took him from cute to handsome. Tall and rangy with not even an ounce of pretension, he was EV's perfect match even if it had taken her half a lifetime to realize it.

As Chloe picked up a scrap of paper containing the next clue, she surveyed the room full of loved ones and felt her heart swell with happiness. Game night was becoming a Friday evening tradition, with all of her favorite people gathered in one place. Tonight's edition they dubbed the 'Almost Blizzard Bowl' since the predicted heavy snowfall had not yet materialized. What was coming down now might have been considered excessive in other parts of the country, but here it was just par for the course.

Veronica, whose voluptuous figure barely evidenced the five children she had birthed, leaned against her husband, Franklin, her face radiating contentment as she absently stroked his arm. Cornflower blue eyes looked up through thick, lowered lashes as her ruby lips stretched into a beguiling smile. Veronica's wild days were behind her —and she had been adventurous to the extreme— and now it was rare to catch her without at least a couple of children clamoring for her attention, or without Mindy, the fourth woman of the group.

Mindy's petite, sylphlike frame belied the yoga and kickboxing-gleaned strength that lay underneath, as did the mischievous smile that she nearly always wore. Mindy, a typical redhead, could go from zero to sixty in about 2.2 seconds. She cast occasional glances at her longtime boyfriend, Jace, who was deep in conversation with Nate across the room.

"V, you're up after me." Chloe tossed the comment over her shoulder and proceeded to draw a bird-like shape and what appeared to be a pile of spaghetti, and watched recognition pass over Nate's face before he correctly guessed 'One Flew Over the Cuckoo's Nest' to her delight. None of the dozens of jobs Chloe had held throughout her thirty-three years had, thankfully, required any level of measurable artistic talent beyond an eye for shape and color.

EV and Dalton, with twenty more years of experience than the rest of the group, were the clear front-runners for the win. It didn't hurt that, save for knitting, EV excelled at just about everything, or that Franklin's tendency toward making questionable guesses thwarted Veronica's superior artistic skills. When, with an economy of line, she rendered a spot-on image of George Washington, Franklin swore it was Indiana Jones.

"And this is for the win," EV took a look at the yellow block on her card and her face flushed a dull red. With swift strokes, she sketched out a series of stacked shapes.

"Blocks? A pyramid?" Dalton called out. EV shook her head. On the top, she roughed out a very hastily drawn stick couple. "Wedding cake?" She added a dress and veil then an arrow pointing toward the male half. "Groom? Husband?" Dalton nailed it half a second before time ran out. He accepted EV's elated high five, then quietly tore the sheet of paper from the oversize tablet, folded it into a bulky square, and stashed it in his pocket.

. . .

"I think they think they're getting away with something, sneaking out to the shed for cigars and man time." Mindy commented with a smirk once the men had vacated and the women were ensconced in the kitchen, sipping wine and laughing like teenagers.

"Let them keep thinking so." EV replied. "Never underestimate the value of the upper hand. Though, to be fair, I'm probably not the authority on how to treat husbands or *boyfriends*, seeing as I haven't been in a long-term relationship for quite some time. By the way, what is a woman in her fifties supposed to call a man anyway? Boyfriend sounds so juvenile..."

"Stud Muffin?" Chloe piped up from her cross-legged position on the kitchen island. When the laughter died down, she continued, "Don't ask me; one of the first thoughts I had after Nate proposed was *thank goodness, I can call him my fiancé now*. Min, what about you—what do you call Jace?"

"I hate to say it, but boyfriend is the best option. You use 'partner', and you have people wondering if you're talking about business, or assuming you're in a same sex relationship. Personally, I don't care what people think, but what I can't stand is the eyebrows that remain raised—either literally or implied—until you clarify with a gender-specific pronoun."

"Companion conjures images of old British ladies for some ungodly reason." Veronica mused. "Beau would be better, but it's so uncommon in the north—and in this decade, for that matter."

"Just don't call him your boo." Chloe teased lightly, trying to imagine the word 'boo' passing EV's lips. "Or your bae. Which, according to social media, is short for 'baby' because apparently that last syllable is too much." She rolled her eyes. "Pretty soon we'll all be speaking in shorthand."

Distaste shot EV's eyebrows up at the word bae. Never. Not ever would that word pass her lips.

Veronica threw an arm around EV's neck and leaned in conspiratorially. "Pretty soon you won't have this problem anyway. Anyone can see where this is headed. According to *Babble & Spin*, you and Dalton ought to be making an announcement anytime now."

Chloe's eyes widened imperceptibly at the reference to her column; she wished she could share her identity with Veronica and Mindy. Chloe firmly believed that secrecy in any form was detrimental to otherwise meaningful relationships, and feared this particular withholding placed a metaphorical wedge in her friendship with the women.

"Believing everything you read in *Babble & Spin* is about the same as basing political opinions on Facebook memes." A small snort escaped Chloe's lips, which EV studiously ignored.

Bait and Snitch is available now, and keep reading for a preview of the free novella you'll get for joining our newsletters.

A Free Story for You

Enjoyed meeting Chloe & EV? They're not the only people who live in our heads!

Sign up for either or both of our newsletters and you'll receive *A Snowball's Chance in Spell*, a prequel novella featuring characters from the *Mag & Clara Balefire Mysteries*, the *Haunted Everly After Mysteries*, and the *Psychic Seasons* series.

Christmas is canceled! Lexi Balefire's faerie godmothers didn't mean to knock Santa Claus and his sleigh out of the sky, but now his reindeer are missing, and it's up to Lexi to find them all before time runs out and Christmas is ruined!

Excerpt from A Snowball's Chance in Spell

L ightning flirted in shadows of the dark clouds hovering over my house when I came home from work the afternoon before my twenty-second Christmas Eve. Nothing unusual there. With three elemental faeries living in the house, weird weather happened all the time. Or rather, every time my temperamental godmothers mounted some sort of snit.

The godmothers idled at snit.

Going back to work wasn't an option. I'd cleared the last match of the year—a lovely couple with a shared affection for online gaming—and I was no coward. When it came to diffusing faerie fights, I consider myself an expert, and this one didn't look like it rated more than a two on the volcano scale.

Yes, you heard right. I measure faerie fights on the scale of whether or not a volcano might erupt in my backyard. Living with faeries is never boring. Occasionally dangerous—especially because I have yet to come into the magic that is my birthright, but never boring.

A quick check proved they'd contained the madness to the inside and/or the backyard. The two feet of snow on the front lawn was still there and still white—you try explaining black snow to your neighbors sometime. I didn't see any winged denizens—fae or otherwise—dotting the roof ridge, or hear any ominous sounds. If not for the fact that lightning is rare in Maine during the winter, and rarer still when confined to a single area, I'd have thought it was a quiet day in the household.

In my head, I downgraded the threat to a level one, and went inside.

For the most part, my place looks like an ordinary, New England style home. Built by my great grandparents, it's the oldest house in a neighborhood that grew up around it when the suburbs expanded into what was once a rural area. Because, I think, the faeries wanted to give me a normal upbringing, they left the house in mostly the same condition it was in when they came to take care of me and only added on a wing for their own use.

I stepped into the front hall expecting...well, just about anything. Did I mention the faeries love holidays? Maybe they don't have them in the faelands, or maybe they do and go overboard there, too. I can't say since I've never been, but I could tell at a glance there were more decorations than there had been when I left.

"Terra!" I yelled, but got no answer. Terra, faerie of earth, held sway over all the flora and fauna found on dry land. She would be the one responsible for the pine boughs twining over anything that held still long enough. Fire faerie, Soleil, contributed by setting sparks of faerie light to twinkle inside the delicate ice bubbles crafted by her sister, Evian, mistress of water. The effect was lovely, but not as lovely as the three women could be when their faces weren't twisted, as they were now, with rage.

I came upon them in their favorite fighting grounds: the kitchen. It looked like I'd caught this one early since there was relatively little damage done so far. Steam rose from a puddle of water at Soleil's feet which I assumed had come from Evian. Vines snaked from between the kitchen tiles to twine around Evian's ankles, and there were a few smoking embers dotting Terra's hair. Nothing more than a minor spat.

Keeping it casual, I asked, "What's going on?"

There's no rhyme or reason to what will settle a fight or send one into the red zone.

Terra turned one granite pink eye in my direction. "This doesn't concern you." The fingers of her left hand twitched and the vines slithered from Evian's ankles to her knees.

Retaliating, Evian conjured a gush of water from thin air, and doused the smoking embers. The scent of pine boughs couldn't compete with the stench of burnt hair, or the pungent funk erupting from the flowers that burst into bloom near her feet.

"Now look," I pointed out to Terra before she conjured something worse. "Evian is trying to help."

"Was not." Evian snapped her fingers and turned Terra's wet hair white with frost, except because the vines were now questing higher, she overshot the mark and doused a few of Soleil's decorative sparkles.

That was the moment I lost control.

Oh, who am I kidding? I never had control.

Soleil let out a screech and lobbed a fireball at Evian, who encased it in a ball of water and batted it toward Terra. I felt scoured clean when Terra called all the dirt and dust in the house to form a layer over the bobbing ball of doom which now resembled a small planet whizzing back toward Soleil.

It might have ended better if I'd have kept my mouth shut, but I didn't.

"You're going to put an eye out with that thing."

The ire of three faeries is a potent thing, but not as potent as a flaming mudball. I ducked, rolled, and hit the latch on the patio door in what I'd like to think was a graceful move. Probably looked like a seal rolling off a rock.

The flaming fireball arced over my head, its warm breeze tossing my hair, and rocketed off into the sky.

Crisis averted. Except, it wasn't. I should have known.

A Snowball's Chance in Spell is only available by signing up for one of our newsletters here:
https://reginawelling.com
https://erinlynnwrites.com

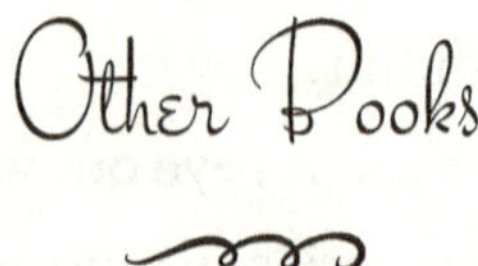

Other Books

If you'd like to meet more people who live rent-free in our heads, here's a list of other series we've written. Our books are all set in fictional towns in Maine, and some characters like to flit back and forth between series. The cast of Psychic Seasons hangs out with Everly and also with Lexi Balefire from the Fate Weaver series. Mag and Clara Balefire are Lexi's grandmother and aunt!

The Psychic Seasons Series
Four women, four love stories, and a whole lot of supernatural surprises. In the quaint town of Oakville, Maine, psychic visions, ghostly whispers, and fate itself conspire to change lives—and hearts—forever

The Haunted Everly After Mysteries

Everly Dupree came home for a fresh start—not a full-time gig solving ghostly murders. But when the dearly departed start demanding justice, what's a reluctant medium to do?

Nell Page: Accidental Investigator
Nell Page owns a bookstore, drinks too much coffee, and has a habit of noticing things she probably shouldn't. With warmth, wit, and an accidental talent for investigating, Nell tackles mysteries that don't always involve murder—but always matter.

Fate Weaver
Lexi Balefire—matchmaker, witch, and accidental fate-weaver—must balance love, magic, and a family legacy of chaos before destiny decides for her!

The Mag and Clara Balefire Mysteries
Sister witches Mag and Clara Balefire move to a sleepy Maine town for a fresh start—only to find themselves conjuring up trouble, solving murders, and keeping their magic under wraps in this charmingly witchy cozy mystery series

Laurel Haven Witches
Four witches, destined by blood and magic, must embrace their power, battle a dark legacy, and surrender to the love that could break the curse—or bind them to it forever.